MONTANA MAVERICKS

Welcome to Big Sky Country, home of the Montana Mavericks! Where free-spirited men and women discover love on the range...

BROTHERS AND BRONCOS

Romance is in the air for the ranchers of Bronco, but someone is watching from the sidelines. A man from the town's past could be behind the mysterious messages, but does he pose a threat to Bronco's future? With their happily-ever-afters at stake, the bighearted cowboys will do what it takes to protect their beloved town— and the women they can't live without!

ONE NIGHT WITH THE MAVERICK

After an unexpected encounter with town veterinarian Felix Sanchez, librarian Shari Lormand does her best not to get her hopes up. But being "just friends" with the widower is harder than she thought. She thinks giving him some time is the best option. However, what if he really needs a little push?

Dear Reader,

Widowed veterinarian Felix Sanchez might not be ready for a new relationship, but that doesn't stop his eighty-five-year-old great-uncle, Stanley, from trying to fix him up. Instead of a night out at Bronco's favorite bar leading *Felix* to love, it's Stanley who falls hard for ninety-five-year-old resident psychic Winona Cobbs. Though Felix *does* unexpectedly meet a woman that night—a wild night neither expected.

Children's librarian Shari Lormand wants marriage and family. She knows the guarded, handsome veterinarian isn't looking for any of that. But they both just might have a lot to learn from the older generation who's been through it all...

I hope you enjoy Felix and Shari's love story—and Stanley and Winona's! I'd love to hear your thoughts and hope you'll visit my website at melissasenate.com for more information about my novels for Harlequin Special Edition.

Warmest regards,

Melissa Senate

One Night
with the Maverick

———

MELISSA SENATE

HARLEQUIN
SPECIAL
EDITION

Special thanks and acknowledgment are given to
Melissa Senate for her contribution to the
Montana Mavericks: Brothers & Broncos miniseries.

Recycling programs
for this product may
not exist in your area.

ISBN-13: 978-1-335-72413-7

One Night with the Maverick

Copyright © 2022 by Harlequin Enterprises ULC

For questions and comments about the quality of this book,
please contact us at CustomerService@Harlequin.com.

Harlequin Enterprises ULC
22 Adelaide St. West, 41st Floor
Toronto, Ontario M5H 4E3, Canada
www.Harlequin.com

Printed in U.S.A.

Melissa Senate has written many novels for Harlequin and other publishers, including her debut, *See Jane Date*, which was made into a TV movie. She also wrote seven books for Harlequin Special Edition under the pen name Meg Maxwell. Her novels have been published in over twenty-five countries. Melissa lives on the coast of Maine with her teenage son; their rescue shepherd mix, Flash; and a lap cat named Cleo. For more information, please visit her website, melissasenate.com.

Books by Melissa Senate

Harlequin Special Edition

Dawson Family Ranch

The Long-Awaited Christmas Wish
Wyoming Cinderella
Wyoming Matchmaker
His Baby No Matter What
Heir to the Ranch

Furever Yours

A New Leash on Love
Home is Where the Hound Is

Montana Mavericks: The Lonelyhearts Ranch

The Maverick's Baby-in-Waiting

Montana Mavericks: The Real Cowboys of Bronco Heights

The Most Eligible Cowboy

Montana Mavericks: Brothers & Broncos

One Night with the Maverick

Visit the Author Profile page
at Harlequin.com for more titles.

For my mother, with all my love.

Chapter One

If thirty-four-year-old widower Felix Sanchez *were* in the market for a relationship, he wouldn't have to bother with dating apps or pricey matchmakers. Not when his eighty-five-year-old great-uncle Stanley spent his days walking up to women without wedding rings in the grocery store to tell them all about his single nephew. *And did I mention he's a doctor? An animal doctor! Bulls, turtles, puppies, he takes care of them all. Tall, handsome fella, too.*

Santiago "Stanley" Sanchez, who'd moved in with the Sanchez family just a few months ago because of his loneliness after losing his wife, never walked away without a phone number for Felix. Not that Felix ever used any of them. His dresser drawer at home was full of slips of paper and business cards. But tonight, Stanley had Felix roped in. His uncle had promised "a very attractive redhead" that they'd be at Doug's bar tonight at seven if she wanted advice on her Pomeranian who chewed up her running shoes, *So you have to come tonight, Felix.*

Grrr. All Felix wanted to do after having partaken in his mother's great cooking—she'd made tamales tonight and he'd eaten five of them—was watch a game, do a little research on some new medications that would be coming into his veterinary office, and call it a night after a long day of tending those bulls and turtles and puppies. A big animal vet who also had clinic hours at the Bronco Heights Animal Hospital, Felix was zonked. He'd started at five thirty this morning—a sick calf— and finally left the clinic at 6:00 p.m.

"You're wearing that?" Stanley said from the doorway of Felix's bedroom. "Can't you put on a nice button-down?"

"We're going to everyone's favorite Bronco Valley dive bar, Uncle Stanley. My University of Montana sweatshirt, growling grizzly mascot and all, will do just fine."

Stanley gave a slight frown. "Did I mention that

lovely redhead who'll be there to talk to you about her little dog is very stylish? A fashion plate."

"Tio. You know I love you. But you've gotta stop with the fix-ups and promises and ruses to put me and single women in the same place at the same time. It's not fair to the women you rope in. I'm not looking for a relationship. It's way too soon."

Stanley waved his hand in the air with a grunt. "It's been three years, Felix. It's time to find love again. And," he added, looking at his watch, which Felix gave him for his birthday last month, "it's almost seven." A big grin split his handsome, lined face. *"Vamos!"*

You go, he wanted to say. But truth be told, he was a little worried about Stanley. Outgoing and warm and funny with his saucy but still G-rated jokes and big laugh, his uncle made friends everywhere he went, yeah. But despite that, Stanley was lonely. He'd lost his dear wife of sixty years just last year, and his grief, the raw pain in his *tio*'s voice when they'd speak by phone, had gotten Felix on a plane a few times to Mexico, where Stanley had still lived, to stay for a few days. Just a few months ago, he'd finally convinced Stanley, with his parents' and siblings' help, to move to the US and start fresh in Montana.

No good deed, he thought, shaking his head with a smile. An hour or two at Doug's, playing a few rounds of darts, nursing a cold beer, didn't sound so bad if it would make his *tio* happy.

"Oh, wait, I forgot something!" Stanley said, hurrying to his room downstairs on the first level. "Meet me by the front door in five."

Felix nodded, grabbed his wallet and keys and was about to head out when his gaze caught on a photo of Victoria. He had just the one now in his bedroom. He'd moved back home soon after he'd lost her to cancer, barely able to slog through a day, let alone take care of the house they'd shared. Had it been three years? Sometimes it felt like *twenty*-three years since he'd been widowed. Sometimes it felt like yesterday.

Downstairs at the door, the smell of his uncle's favorite aftershave overpowered the delicious lingering aroma of the tamales and rice they'd had for dinner.

"Last chance to change your shirt," Stanley said with hope all over his face.

"Nah, I'm good."

"Good-looking!" Stanley said with a laugh and three little punches on Felix's arm.

Felix laughed, too. His uncle's goofy jokes and good-humored kindness were infectious, even when Felix just wanted to brood.

"And no doubt your soon-to-be new girlfriend,"

Stanley added, "the pretty redhead with the Pomeranian will think so, too."

Felix shook his head and headed for his SUV, till Stanley headed for his own pickup.

Stanley hopped in the driver's seat. "I'll drive tonight. It's one of those gorgeous early fall nights. Sixty-four degrees. Nice breeze. I want to roll the windows down and crank up the mariachi."

Which he did, singing along to an old CD as they drove over to Doug's in Bronco Valley, not far from the Sanchez home in the same part of town.

As they headed in, an '80s-era Bon Jovi song was blaring from the old-timey jukebox. The bar was pretty crowded tonight. An easel by the door had a sign noting that Bronco's resident psychic, Winona Cobbs, would be giving free readings from 6:00 until 7:15 p.m. A few times a year, Winona, who had her own psychic shop in town, held events at Doug's.

Felix had no interest in a psychic reading, even if he'd heard Winona, whose readings were short and sweet, sometimes just one line, *always* got it right. Felix had no interest in what was coming. He'd had his share of bad news coming to fruition.

He and Stanley took two seats at the long bar, and within moments, a redhead, indeed pretty and stylish, had materialized in the open seat beside him. Stanley disappeared with his quarters to the jukebox, naturally. Felix listened to the woman's troubles with her Pomeranian, Peaches, gave her some advice about keeping her sneakers behind closed doors in a closet and giving Peaches toys with a similar texture.

"I hope you make house calls," the woman said in a throaty purr and rested her hand on his arm.

Felix went for honesty. "For emergencies, but I should add that I'm a recent widower and I'm not ready to date."

The part about being widowed always seemed to let women know his lack of interest wasn't personal, and sometimes he even made a friend out of his uncle's matchmaking ways. The redhead left, and the next time he looked over at her table, she was deep in conversation with a rancher.

The bartender, Doug Moore himself, took his and Stanley's order, plunking down their bottles of beers. Stanley turned around on his barstool until he was facing out, sipping his beer, and keeping his eyes on the dartboard for when it would be free.

"Now there's a woman who knows how to live," Stanley said, sitting up straighter, and—if Felix wasn't mistaken—sucking in his belly. Stanley pointed his beer bottle at white-haired Winona Cobbs, who sat at a round table near the back of the room likely so she could conduct her readings privately and away from the blare of the jukebox.

"I like her style. I surely do." Stanley seemed riveted by Winona, his dark brown eyes getting all twinkly.

Felix smiled. Winona Cobbs, wearing a purple cowboy hat, silver fringed pantsuit and purple cowboy boots, was ninety-five years old. An older woman even by eighty-five-year-old Stanley's standards.

"Ooh, that man just left her table," Stanley said, hopping off the barstool. "I'm going over for a reading. You should too, Felix."

"You go ahead," he told his uncle. Felix had always been superstitious—enough to avoid walking under open ladders or crossing the paths of black cats, which also happened to be his secret favorites, and he knocked on wood if he ever proclaimed anything. Plus, he really had heard enough stories about Winona's readings coming true for people to know she did have psychic gifts. But he'd rather his future remain a mystery. It was better not to know.

"I'll need a proper introduction," Stanley said, giving his throat a gentle clear and again sucking in his belly, not that he had much of a beer gut. Stanley Sanchez was six feet tall and robust and liked to wear black leather vests over Western-style shirts, a black cowboy hat and cowboy boots. His look was one of the reasons everyone in town had taken to him so easily and fast. He fit in.

Felix took a slug of his beer, then another, and walked over to Winona's table with his uncle. He knew her only casually from around town.

"Miss Cobbs," Felix began.

Winona's sharp gaze beelined to him. "Oh, my," she said. "Your life is an open book, but I'm afraid there's nothing there for me to read."

Felix frowned. What the heck did that mean?

"But *this* face," she added, staring at Stanley warmly—and with interest—"this face tells a whole story."

Stanley grinned. "I can't wait to hear what's in store for me, Miss Winona." He sat down, never taking his eyes off the nonagenarian. "Felix, bring me my beers, will you?"

"Sure," Felix said, but he doubted his uncle even heard him. He was already chatting up a storm with the white-haired psychic, complimenting her outfit and mentioning that purple was his new favorite color.

Oh, Lord. His uncle was *flirting*.

And Winona Cobbs, who had a stoic, serious way about her, was flirting back. Felix even heard an "Oh, you!" on a giggle with a dainty wave of her hand.

Never, not once, had Felix seen his uncle flirt with any of the elderly widows in Bronco. He must be truly smitten with Winona.

Since no introductions were necessary at this point, Felix went back over to the bar, grabbed his uncle's beer and set it down on the table, neither party looking up from their conversation. *You go*, he said silently to Tio Stanley as he went back to the bar and sat down. A guy grabbed the open spot on his right. So much for saving his uncle's seat, but it was pretty crowded and Stanley didn't look like he'd be getting up from Winona's table any-time soon. It was past seven fifteen now and her reading event had ended with Stanley.

"Ugh, I don't even like to sit *next to* the haunted barstool," a woman's voice said. She moved the last available stool, the one to his left, a bit closer to his and sat down.

Him, too. The Death Seat, as the locals called it, was legendary in Bronco. It was about a foot away from hers, the last one, and cordoned off with rope entwined with crime scene tape. No one dared to sit in it, no matter how crowded the place was.

He turned to see a pretty woman he recognized from around town—and from school. She had long, curly strawberry blond hair, green eyes be-hind round tortoiseshell glasses and a warm smile. He tried to come up with her name, but drew a blank. If Stanley were over here he'd likely compli-ment her style just as he had Winona's. She wore a long dress with squares and circles all over it and a satin sash around her hips, a necklace with tiny painted ceramic books dangling off it and tall red leather boots.

"I hear you," he said, not even wanting to *look* at the haunted barstool. "I'll switch with you so I'm closer to it, though."

"Would you?" she asked, her green eyes lighting up. "I'm a little superstitious."

It wouldn't be gallant or manly to say *me, too* or *I didn't think you'd take me up on it*, so he switched seats. Apparently, anyone who'd ever sat on the Death Seat immediately had trouble befall them. A breakup. An air conditioner falling out a second-story window and landing on their foot, narrowly missing their head. The worst flu ever. And a few years ago: Death. A man named Bobby Stone had sat on the Death Seat—and fell off a cliff a few days later during a hike in the mountains.

Still, once every few months some drunken loudmouth leaped over the tape and made a show of sitting on the stool, proclaiming the legend of the haunted barstool total baloney. And then, a half hour later, the person would be by the jukebox, trip over something and chip a tooth. No, Felix wouldn't sit on that barstool for a hundred grand.

He finished a second beer, not even sure when he'd started on it. But now he wanted something different. A whiskey, straight up. Doug plunked it down, then took the woman's order. She ordered a craft beer.

The woman's presence, so close to him, reminded him of Victoria. He was sure they'd been friends. Or friendly. He remembered the long strawberry blond hair, Victoria often commenting that she'd give anything for that color and texture, even though her dark hair was gorgeous. And the eyeglasses, though maybe not those same ones.

Sarah. Sandra. Stephanie. Selina. Something with an *S...* He could smell her faint perfume, a sandalwood tinge to it that he liked. He sucked down his drink and figured he'd go grab his uncle and they'd head home, but when he turned around, he saw Stanley sitting *beside* Winona now, not across from her like before, and they were both staring into each other's eyes and talking.

Had his uncle picked up a woman in Doug's super-dive bar? An older woman? Felix shook his head with a grin. *Hey. More power to you, Tio.*

Felix turned back around, eyeing the plate of buffalo wings and blue cheese dressing Doug had placed down in front of the strawberry blonde. He'd had so many tamales that he wasn't hungry, but man, those wings smelled good.

"Want one, Felix?" the woman offered, pushing the plate a little to the right.

She knew *his* name. Now he felt even worse

that he didn't remember hers. He wondered what else she knew about him. That he was a widower? That he was a veterinarian? That he didn't go out much? Or usually drink much?

Yet here was, sucking down his fourth of the night like it was water.

What was wrong with him?

You're alone. In a crowded bar. Realizing that your formerly wonderful life is behind you, not ahead of you.

He sighed and took a wing, swiping it in the blue cheese.

"Thanks," he said. He took a bite. Delicious.

She smiled. The kind of smile that lit up a face that was already *too* pretty.

He felt someone come up behind him, stopping between him and the blonde. It was Everlee Roberts, whom everyone called Evy, a waitress at Doug's. "Hey, Felix. Did you know your uncle just left with Winona Cobbs?"

He stared at Evy. "What? They left?" He glanced at the table. Empty, just like both his uncle's beers.

"No worries," Evy told him as if reading his mind. "They left on foot." He strained his neck to look out the window and saw his uncle's truck still parked in the lot. But no sign of Stanley. Or Winona.

Which meant his uncle had stranded him here

since Tio had the keys. Great. Doug's was a quick drive from his house, but still a good four miles away, and two beers and two whiskey shots had made him a little tipsy, he realized. No one wanted to see their veterinarian, big animal or turtle, stumbling home from a dive bar.

He could call his dad, but then remembered his parents had left for the movies not long before he and Stanley had gone out. Darn. He could bother one of his siblings but he'd never hear the end of how he let Uncle Stanley disappear into the night with a woman—a psychic, no less, who clearly had to know the night would end well.

He wasn't sure his uncle wanted any of *that* to be family knowledge, so he ignored his phone. There was always a rideshare, he thought, signaling to Doug for another whiskey. No, make that a draft beer.

Two were set before him.

He drank one, thinking about old times. Thinking about his old life. And thinking about what the hell the nice-smelling, green-eyed blonde woman's name could possibly be.

Sera. Serena. Sally. Suki. None of those were right.

Sensual. That she was.

As she and Evy started chatting, something about a story hour at the library, he started on the second beer. His *second* second beer but his sixth drink. Felix realized he didn't need to know the blonde's name. It wasn't like they'd be flirting up a storm the way his uncle and Winona had. Let alone leaving together, for heaven's sake. He wouldn't be leaving with a woman from a bar for a long, long time. Even if it had been a long, long time since he'd lost Victoria. He was fine on his own.

Just fine. But that didn't stop him from thinking about how they'd so excitedly decided to start a family just days before her diagnosis with cancer. How walking past a playground, how seeing a baby or toddler at the clinic during an appointment for the family pet made his heart clench.

Those times would remind him his heart wasn't numb like he thought. And that he'd never be ready to know the strawberry blonde's name.

Shari Lormand mentally shook her head at the gorgeous man sitting next to her, drinking away his sorrows at Doug's bar. She rarely saw Felix Sanchez out, but had been aware of him for years, since high school, when she'd had a secret crush on him. She'd been too shy to start a conversation with him back then. And the morning she'd marched into school determined to at least say hi, he'd been holding hands with a beautiful dark-haired girl named Victoria. So much for Shari and Felix becoming the couple in her dreams.

And now, being single, *very* single at thirty-four, Shari was aware of every eligible bachelor in town, and Felix Sanchez, widower of three years, was *not* eligible. He was clearly not over losing his wife, not that he should be, of course. He just happened to stand out in town since he was so damned good-looking with those intense hazel eyes and dark thick hair that was just slightly long for a veterinarian and made him look a bit like a rebel. Shari always noticed him when she saw him around Bronco.

"Oh, Felix, I have to thank you again," Evy said, collecting empty glasses from the bar, including a few of Felix's. "Archie is doing really well now. Wes and I can't thank you enough for saving our puppy."

Shari glanced at Felix. She remembered how worried Evy had been about her now-fiancé's puppy, Archie, who'd been swatted by a mama bear protecting her cubs back in July. Not only had Felix saved the adorable pup's life, but he'd apparently called a few times to check in on how Wes Abernathy, Evy and Evy's young daughter were doing during the recovery and rehab since they were all so worried about Archie. That Felix was one of the good guys wasn't in doubt. He just wasn't *available*.

"Really glad to hear it," Felix said.

As Evy got called away to take a table's order, Shari thought about making a quick getaway. She'd come for wings and a beer and to drown her own sorrows, but being so close to a guy like Felix—who ticked every box on her list of what she wanted in a man, in a husband, in the father of her future children—made her feel even more alone. She should go home, draw a bath, pour in some of the scented bubbles she'd gotten as a gift, and forget about how lonely she was. She hated that word *lonely*. But between wanting to get married and all the terrible dates and false starts at relationships, Shari Lormand, children's librarian with an otherwise rich and full life, was lonely.

Her mother's call a half hour ago had left her weirdly unsettled, which was really why she'd stopped in at Doug's, needing…something. A little company, a little noise from voices and the juke-box. Her mom lived in Denver, where the Lormand family had moved after Shari graduated from high school because her father had been transferred for work. Shari had gone to college in Denver, loving city life after growing up in a small town like Bronco. She'd dated a little, had a couple of year-long relationships, and figured she'd meet her

Mr. Right soon. She thought she had when she was twenty-six—Paul, a medical intern who was smart and focused and liked to cook for her in his little free time. When he'd used his long hours and stress as the reason why he was putting off proposing—for five years—Shari had believed it all because she'd been unable to bear believing otherwise. That he just didn't want to marry *her*. That became apparent when she gave him something of an ultimatum, a really weak one: *If you're not able to tell me you want to marry me by the end of the year, I'll have to think about moving on.* Paul broke up with her that night.

And he married someone else a few months later. He'd actually sent her a thank-you card for giving him that ultimatum, which had made him realize he just didn't love her in that way and when he'd met his wife, he'd known she was the one right away. *So thank you, Shari, from both of us.*

Shari had been so hurt, so mad at her own inability to see the truth for years, that she'd left Denver and headed back home to warm, sweet, cozy Bronco, Montana. She'd wanted the familiarity of her hometown and all the comforts that went with it. And now, three years later, Bronco *was* comforting. She loved her job at the library. She had really wonderful friends, like Evy. But being strung along like that and then dumped had made her wary and she was probably a little *too* guarded on dates. The few relationships she'd had hadn't gone anywhere. Now here she was, still single—and thirty-four. And now her biological clock was ticktocking and she wanted children, adding to the pressure.

Tonight, her mother had been filling her in on life and gossip in Denver and the family, then casually mentioned seeing Shari's ex with his pregnant wife and toddler daughter. That had put Shari in a mood, to say the least.

And spicy wings, a cheap beer—or two—and a hot but unavailable man right beside her hadn't helped much.

She and Evy had talked endlessly about the state of Shari's love life, her friend assuring her the man of her dreams was right around the corner. Evy was the single mother of a darling four-year-old named Lola and over the summer had unexpectedly found true love with a great guy, Wes Abernathy—a wealthy rancher who was great with kids and loved dogs, as Evy did. Shari was taken by little Lola, who loved coming to the children's library events. The sweet girl made her so wistful about how much she wanted a child of her own.

To the point that she'd stared exploring her options. If she wasn't going to get married and have a baby the traditional way, there were other ways to become a mother. Sperm donor and IVF. Adoption. She'd just started looking into it all, and it was so overwhelming that she hadn't gotten very far.

Because you want what you've dreamed of since you were a teenager. To fall in love. Marry the man you want to grow old and gray with on your porch, sipping sweet tea, an old dog or two beside you. Have three or four kids. Shari loved the idea of a big family, but now she'd be very happy with one child.

Two pretty young women came in and settled on the barstools on the other side of Shari.

"Aren't you a veterinarian?" one of the women asked over her to Felix, a hand twirling her silky blond hair. "I'm thinking of adopting a puppy and would love some tips for a first-timer."

Oh, brother, Shari thought, sure the woman's interest was not in a puppy. She inwardly sighed and pulled a novel out of her tote bag. She'd finish her wings, another chapter of the absorbing romantic suspense, then get the heck out of here. She couldn't help but smile when she noticed Felix was not flirting back. He was polite but so clearly not interested that the women got up and moved to the group of guys playing darts. She heard a "Well, *hello* ladies" from one of them and rolled her eyes. Everyone was having fun but her. And Felix, apparently.

"Last wing is yours, if you want it," she said to Felix. "I've gotta get home. Busy, busy night ahead of me."

"Oh, yeah?" he asked, taking the wing and swiping it in the dressing. "Working on something?"

"Hot bath, Netflix, more of this book," she said, then felt her cheeks turn red. Had she just lied in his face about being busy and then told him the stark truth of her real next few hours? She quickly shoved her book in her bag.

"Sounds like a perfect night to me," he said. "But I'm stranded here." He explained about arriving with his uncle, who had immediately gotten very chatty with Winona Cobbs and left with her.

"Wow!" Shari said, utterly charmed. "That's really sweet." And inspiring. She was pretty sure that Winona was well into her nineties. And now even Winona had a love life.

"Except my uncle has the keys," Felix said. "And his truck is right there," he added, pointing out the window. "Mocking me."

Shari smiled. "Come on. I'll give you a ride home."

"Thanks—" he started, then seemed deep in concentration, as if trying very hard to remember her name.

She scowled as she stood up, careful to not even touch the caution tape around the haunted barstool with her tote bag or elbow lest she add more bad luck to her life. "You don't know my name, do you?" she accused lightheartedly, eyes narrowed. Her voice might be light but *humph*—how dare he not remember her?

"To be very honest," he said, standing up, too, "I've had a few drinks. I can't remember my own middle name. But I'm pretty sure your first name starts with an *S*."

Okay, that was something. "Shari Lormand." She stuck out her hand and he shook it, smiling at her with that killer smile, his dark eyes focused on her. Whoo boy. She felt the effect of his penetrating gaze. She wondered what he was thinking.

Nah, she knew. *Woman in a weird dress, lace-up boots and a book necklace—reading a book at a bar, no less—is not my type.* The problem was that Shari was never anyone's type. Evy always told Shari she was her own woman and one day she'd find her other half, but it was taking annoyingly longer than Shari wanted. Back in high school she'd been the typical plain Jane, but she'd slowly developed her own style, with a bit of bohemian flair, and though it might be different, she liked who she was.

"Shari!" he said, snapping his finger as those hazel eyes lit up. "Yes, Shari, of course. I do remember you."

She nodded. "I was so sorry to hear about your loss."

His lips clamped tight and he gave her something of a nod.

She grabbed her car keys and they headed out of the bar. "What do you think your uncle and Winona are doing right now?" Her cheeks burned again. "Wait, forget I asked."

He laughed. "I have no doubt what they're doing. My great-uncle is a total romantic. He probably asked if Winona would like to go to Lookout Point for the view of the mountains, the valley and the stars. He might have sung her so many old mariachi songs that she got up and ran far, far away a half hour ago."

She grinned and opened her car door, unlocking the passenger side. "I wouldn't be so sure, Felix. I sure wouldn't mind someone crooning mariachi songs in my ear."

"I might just be tipsy enough," he said.

Oh, wouldn't that be nice, she thought, suddenly imagining him kissing her. Crooning. Kissing her. Crooning.

He directed her to his house and explained that he'd moved into the family home after he was widowed and that Stanley had joined them a few months ago. "It's usually crowded with

Sanchezes—my siblings are often around, too—
but tonight, everyone's out for the evening."

She was about to turn into the driveway of the
modest Bronco Valley house, admiring the flower
boxes and well-kept lawn, when she realized it was
roped off since it had clearly just been repaved.
She pulled up along the curb just past the house.
"Well, this is you." *Too soon*, she thought wistfully.

"I could use a cup of coffee or two," he said,
taking off his seat belt. "Happy to make you a cup
as a thank-you for the ride."

Every nerve ending sizzled. Had Felix Sanchez,
all six feet two of muscled hotness and smarts and
niceness, just invited her in—supposedly for a cup
of coffee? She usually wasn't one to flatter herself, but c'mon. You did not invite someone into
your home unless you didn't want your time together to end.

And then what? she asked herself. A one-night
stand, which was all it would be, because Felix was
hardly interested in dating, let alone a relationship.
She knew that just from tonight, from the very attractive women he'd shown no interest in. And he
hadn't flirted with her once.

Between that and the fact that she wasn't someone who could handle a one-night stand, she
smiled tightly and said that it was getting late.

"Oh, okay," he said, looking a bit glum. "You're

just so easy to talk to. You've made me laugh to-night and I haven't done much of that in a while."

"Yeah, me, either," she said. "Not that I've lost someone very close to me. But I know heartache."

"One cup, then," he said, tilting his head. "My mother makes the most incredible churros and chocolate caramel sauce to dip them into. There are two left from dessert tonight. One for me and one for you. You don't want to miss that."

"I really don't," she said with a smile, almost unable to pull her eyes off his face, his lips, his strong jawline. The man radiated hotness. "Okay, sure, one cup—and a churro." She undid her seat belt.

And just like that, Shari Lormand was walking beside Felix Sanchez into his house. His empty house. Hope chased away any trace of loneliness. Maybe something would happen tonight.

She'd take it one kiss at a time.

Chapter Two

As they headed inside the house, Felix had nothing more on his mind than the coffee, a churro and talking more to the easygoing Shari. Yes, she was very pretty and he *had* noticed her curves in her dress. And she smelled so good—the slightly spicy perfume was intoxicating. And he was already intoxicated.

Once inside, Felix called out an *hola* to see if anyone was actually home. Silence.

"Just you and me," he said.

Shari smiled, his gaze shooting to her plush pink-red lips. "This is your family, right?" she asked, moving to the wall of framed photographs lining the hallway. There were at least fifty of various sizes, the Sanchezes at various ages. She recognized several of them from around town, his mother and sister, particularly.

He stood beside her, pointing. "My parents, my grandparents, there's my uncle Stanley catching his first fish in Montana this past June. My two brothers, Dylan and Dante, my sister Sofia wearing one of her own fashion designs, and that's my sister Camilla standing in front of the restaurant she owns in Bronco Valley—The Library."

"I work there. The actual library, I mean. I'm the children's librarian."

He winced. Children. When would the word or the sight of a baby stop making his chest ache? Luckily, Shari hadn't been looking at him just then; she was smiling at the series of photos of Uncle Stanley on a hiking trip the family had taken when he'd first arrived.

"I'm envious of your big family. I'm an only child," she explained. "And so were my parents. No aunts, uncles or cousins. And both sets of grandparents are gone." Her expression seemed wistful, her gaze still on the photos. "You're so lucky to have this big beautiful family and a great-uncle to go to Doug's with. I wish I had a wise great-aunt to talk to about life over wings and two-for-one-draft beers."

"Uncle Stanley *is* plenty wise," he said, smiling at a photo of him and the five Sanchez kids outside a taco stand on a trip to Mexico when they were teenagers. He *was* lucky to have his great family. "How about a dog or cat? Goldfish?"

She shook her head. "Just me. I've thought about adopting a pet, but I work full-time. One of these days, maybe."

He envisioned Shari Lormand coming home from work after a long day at the library in the children's section, toddlers pulling out books into a growing pile on the floor. No one waiting for her at home, no one to greet her or rub her shoulders, hand her a glass of wine. Or a churro. When he'd lost Victoria he'd been unable to bear living alone. It was a reminder of his grief. His family had saved him.

"How about that churro?" he asked.

Once again her smile lit up her face. "Sounds very good."

He led the way into the tidy kitchen. He lifted the lid off the cake plate, but found only crumbs. "Uncle Stanley!" he said with narrowed eyes. He laughed and shook his head. "The man eats us out of house and home. Why did I think there would actually be leftover dessert? I apologize. If I didn't have, like, five drinks I would have remembered that."

Shari laughed. "No worries. That's the thing about living alone. Every last cookie is mine."

Alone, alone, alone. The word echoed in his head. He'd been alone for three years. The opposite of what Victoria had wanted for him in her final wishes. On her last day, in the morning, when he hadn't known she'd be gone by that evening, she'd said, *I want you to find love again, Felix. I don't want you to be alone. Promise me.*

He promised. Of course, he promised. Only because there was no time component. His promise would be good in ten years or twenty. Maybe when he was eighty-five he'd be ready like Stanley clearly was.

Anytime his family brought up the subject of him dating, which was unfortunately too often, and he said he wasn't ready, one would ask what that meant, what *ready* would feel like. Felix would shrug, but recently Stanley had answered that question for his mother. *He'll feel like his heart is opening like a spring flower instead of closed like a fist.* Felix had asked him if he himself felt that way, and Stanley said sometimes he did and sometimes he didn't. Grief, Felix knew, was complicated—and individual. So was *ready.*

"I'll make us a pot of coffee," Felix said, turning to open the cabinet. "Or," he said, turning to face her, "we could have a glass of my father's incredible sangria."

"I love sangria. Just half a glass, though."

He grabbed the pitcher from the refrigerator, the sangria topped with sliced oranges, pineapple, pears and peaches. He poured out two glasses then handed one to her and leaned back against the counter.

She took a sip and smiled. "This is great."

"It's why I haven't moved out in three years," he said, taking a long drink. "Between my mother's cooking and my father's drink-making skills and my long days, I'm set."

She took a sip, then another. "I hear ya. I'd love to come home to a delicious dinner and a glass of wine and a kiss. But my romantic prospects haven't worked out."

"You should do what I do," he said. "Just remove yourself from that world. No dates. No expectations."

She seemed to think about that for a moment. "But then there's no home-cooked linguini carbonara and garlic bread and that glass of wine waiting for me after a long day at the library."

"True, but there's no heartache. No loss. No falling to your knees and sobbing in agony and three years later, walking around kind of…removed from the rest of the world." He sucked down the rest of the sangria and poured himself half a glass more. What the hell was he saying? *Why* was he saying it? He didn't know this woman. Even though he kind of felt like he did.

"Is that how you feel?" she asked, reaching over to squeeze his hand for a moment. He liked the contact, but it was gone too soon. So warm, so soft. That intoxicating perfume just a bit closer for those two seconds.

"I'm used to being on my own. While living with my family. Best of both worlds for me right now, so I'm good."

"You must be pretty set on staying single since I noticed women flirting with you at Doug's," she said.

"It drives my family nuts that I never respond to any of that. My parents, siblings and Uncle Stanley all try very hard to turn my single status around. They think I should be finding someone new, starting over. But who the hell wants to go through that again?"

"The dating or the possibilities of heartache?" she asked, her eyes serious on his.

He topped off her glass with more sangria. "Both."

She sipped her drink, his gaze on her lush lips. So pink-red and full. "I wonder what's wrong with me, then. I got really burned by my last relationship and yet here I am, still hoping." She froze and her eyes widened. "I don't mean right here, right now. With you," she added fast. "Just in general."

"So you're looking to get married."

She nodded. "And have a baby. I'm thirty-four and the clock is ticking on me. To be honest, I'm exploring all my options. Just at the starting point." She waved her free hand in the air and took another sip. "Ahh, let's change the subject." She pointed at his sweatshirt. "How about those Montana Grizzlies?"

He smiled gently, full of unexpected tenderness for her. He turned away for a moment and drank more of his sangria. She wanted a husband and a child. A family. Even if he *was* looking to date casually, which he wasn't, she couldn't be a part of his life with those hopes and dreams. His heart, what was left of it, was shuttered closed.

But then why was he noticing the flecks of green and brown in Shari's pretty hazel eyes? The sweep of her lashes? He liked her elegant nose, and her full lips. He liked her dress and the book necklace and the red boots. And her hair…why did he have the urge to run his fingers through that silky mass of strawberry blond, his hand running along the back of her neck?

"I'm glad you were sitting next to me tonight at Doug's," he said, aware of how close they were—

the distance between the counters they leaned against in the kitchen. "I haven't spent time with someone who isn't a relative or a patient's human in a long time."

"I'm glad, too," she whispered, setting down her empty glass. "Thank you for the sangria."

"Thank *you*," he said, not quite sure what he was thanking her for. But something. Something big and small.

He set his glass down, too, unable to drag his eyes off her face. He stepped closer, suddenly wondering what it would be like to kiss her. *I'm a little drunk*, he thought. *Of course my inhibitions are lowered. I'm not thinking straight.* Yet he felt in full control of himself. He knew exactly what he was doing as he stepped closer still, reaching a hand to touch a tendril of her hair. "So pretty," he said, his gaze on her hair.

He heard her intake of breath, saw her smile slightly fade as she looked at him, her eyes full of…desire. Yearning.

She stepped a bit closer, too. "I like yours, too. So dark and such contrast with your hazel eyes."

He leaned his face toward hers. Slowly. Looking right at her.

She leaned hers toward his.

And when their lips met—fire. Felix felt those sparks all over his body. Then his arms were suddenly around her, his hands now on either side of her face as he deepened the kiss. *More, more, more*, he thought.

He pulled back for a moment. "I want to kiss you all night. I want more than that. But as I said, I'm not looking…not ready for a…" He trailed off, not wanting to ruin this, not wanting her to leave, not wanting to stop kissing her. But he wasn't a jerk, either. Tipsy or not. He took another step backward and stumbled a bit, and she caught him.

"Mmm," he said. "You smell so good. You *feel* so good."

"How about I help you upstairs to your room and then I'll be going," she said. "When a man tells me he's not ready, I now believe him instead of sticking around for five years and getting my heart smashed."

He tilted his head. The heartache she'd mentioned. He certainly didn't want to add to it.

Suddenly, his head began to spin a little. Then a little more.

He felt her move to his side and take his arm. She led him up the stairs.

"Second door on the right," he said.

She opened the door and his gaze landed on his bed. King-sized. Four-poster. Imported from Mexico. Heavenly down comforter and fluffy pillows. She led him over and he sat down, and she was taking off his boots. Kneeling in front of him. Making him imagine all kinds of things.

"Don't go, Shari Lormand," he said, tilting up her chin. "Maybe we could have just tonight. This unexpected rendezvous."

"Just tonight," she repeated, staring at him. Staring hard, those hazel eyes working. *She's making a decision*, he realized. *Should I stay or should I go?*

Decision made. Because suddenly she'd whipped her glasses off like a female Clark Kent, set them on the end table and slowly unbuttoned his shirt, her eyes on his the entire time. She flung it to a chair, then unsnapped his jeans. He fell back on the bed, his feet on the rug so that she'd have an easier time shrugging them off him.

"Black boxer briefs. Nothing sexier," she whispered. This close up, she could see them. And the outline of him underneath. He kicked his jeans off, and they landed on top of the lamp on the end table.

"Nothing sexier than *you*," he whispered, pulling her up onto him.

And then they were kissing again. All thought left his head, blessedly, and he just *felt*. Her hands on his skin, in his hair, across his chest, her lips on his, trailing kisses down his chest, a warm soft hand inside those boxer briefs, exploring.

She stepped back and unzipped her boots and took off her socks. Even her feet were incredibly sexy. In the three seconds that she moved to unzip her dress, Felix felt his head spinning again. Then it stopped. His eyes grew so heavy that he couldn't keep them open to see Shari's beautiful form once the dress fell down her body and pooled on the floor. His last conscious thought was that she wore the sexiest white cotton bra he'd ever seen.

And then he felt the pull of sleep overtake him.

Felix was out cold. Fast asleep. And Shari was standing beside his bed, in her bra and underwear, her dress at her feet. She eyed his jeans on top of the lamp.

What the hell had she been thinking?

Until he passed out, he'd been ready for sex, but not ready for a relationship. She'd heard him loud and clear. But in that moment, when she could have left or stayed, she'd thought, *oh, just stay and go for it. Have a new experience. Just don't expect anything in the morning.*

Like she wouldn't have. She was Shari Lormand, *expecter.*

You're damned lucky he fell asleep, she told herself. Because she absolutely would have slept with him. And then she'd have had to slink out after because it wasn't like she could sleep over.

And in the morning, he'd remember that he'd spent the night with someone, that woman from the bar, and he'd feel like hell because she knew he was a gentleman. A gentleman told a woman he wasn't ready for a relationship before they went too far. He'd even had the decency to fall asleep before she could get her bra and undies off.

Shari sighed and grabbed her eyeglasses, shoved them on and then got into her dress, contorting her arms backward to zip it. She glanced around for anything of hers. Her necklace was still on. Where did her socks go? Ah, there they were, flung off by the bedside table. She grabbed them, then sat down on the edge of the bed, so aware of the hot sleeping man stretched out on his back, one arm flung up behind his head, and pulled on her boots.

The walk of shame. She got up, smoothed her hair, grabbed her tote bag and headed for the door. But when she opened it, she heard the unmistakable sound of a key turning in a lock downstairs. Then voices. Two voices, a man and a woman. Then the door shutting.

"It's so quiet!" the woman said. "I guess Felix and Stanley are still out."

"I'll bet Stanley is getting Felix into some kind of good trouble," the man's voice said.

Then she heard footsteps. Then: "*Dios Mio!*

Who ate the last two churros? I was saving them for us after the movies!"

Shari would have smiled if she were not standing stock-still, hand still on the doorknob, eyes wide. She slowly closed the door, her heart beating way too fast. His parents were home and how was she supposed to leave? Just waltz down the stairs with her mussed hair and clearly kissed lips and flushed cheeks and say, *Oh, hi, I hear ya on the churros, we were hoping to have them, too.*

She leaned against the back of Felix's bedroom door and let out a breath. Now what?

She'd wait for them to come upstairs and go into their bedroom and close the door. Then she'd sneak down the stairs like a cat and hurry out the door. Yes, that was the plan. Okay.

She waited. A few minutes passed. She could hear them chatting downstairs. Laughter. The sound of a song. Spanish, she was pretty sure.

"You devil!" she heard his mother say.

Shari had a feeling they were dancing.

This might be a while. She could pull out her book, but could she really concentrate on one sentence? Probably not.

She sat on the edge of Felix's bed, looking at his beautiful, peaceful face. She sighed again, wishing she could curl up beside him, move his arm over her.

She strained to hear downstairs. Music was still playing. Footsteps. But not coming upstairs.

She lay down as close to the edge of the bed as possible, her booted feet dangling off, her arms folded over her chest. She removed her eyeglasses, setting them on the table again. Any minute now, she'd hear them come upstairs, close their door, and she could flee.

At least she'd have a good story for Evy tomorrow, she thought, closing her eyes with a smile.

But when she opened her eyes, sunshine was coming through the filmy curtains on the window. Disoriented for a moment, Shari sat up, no idea where she was.

And then she looked to the left. She practically jumped. Felix was facing her, still sleeping. The comforter down around his belly button. Oh, my. His chest really was amazing. And the line of dark hair down his stomach…

And then *his* eyes opened.

He stared at her, then bolted up. He glanced at his alarm clock on the bedside table: 6:52 a.m. "Did we…" he prompted. "I hate that I have to ask." He shook his head and scrubbed a hand over his face.

"No," she said, scrambling off the bed, sliding on her glasses and looking for her socks again.

Ah—they were stuffed inside her boots. "We might have, but you fell asleep."

"No reflection on you," he said—awkwardly.

She sat at his desk chair and put on her socks and her boots, so aware that he was watching her. "I would have left when you passed out, but when I got to your bedroom door, your parents had just come home. And I waited for them to come upstairs and go into their room, but they never did and I guess I fell asleep."

He shook his head and for a moment she was mesmerized by the sexy tangle of his mussed dark hair. "I don't usually have more than one beer. I don't know what the heck came over me last night."

She could feel her cheeks pinkening. *Awkward.* "Well, I really need to get home and get ready for work." She dashed over to the door. "Well, bye!" she added, then opened the door and peered out, looking both ways. The coast was clear. She didn't hear a sound from downstairs.

"Wait," he whispered. "I—"

She turned and stared at him. *I what?* No—she didn't want to know. She was almost sure of it.

Clutching her tote bag, she hurried out and ran down the stairs. Her eyes widened as she heard a woman's voice upstairs softly singing a song in Spanish. Shari was about to rush for the front door, but froze on the bottom step when she saw two guys, their backs to her, in the kitchen, looking through the refrigerator and cabinets and chatting about their hope that *Mami* would make her incredible chocolate chip pancakes for them. Must be Felix's brothers, stopping over for a home-cooked breakfast. Of all the mornings!

She held her breath and hurriedly tiptoed toward the front door. Clear! She raced out and across the lawn to her car at the curb. Only when she closed the door did she breathe. She drove away, her heart pounding.

Suddenly, she didn't want to share this experience with Evy. Or think about it too much. Because she knew she'd never hear from Felix Sanchez again. Yeah, maybe he'd track her down and apologize for falling asleep on her or her being trapped in his room all night. Or racing out of his house at just past sunrise to make the drive of shame.

Except as Shari drove home to her condo in Bronco Heights, she didn't feel ashamed in the slightest. She felt slightly exhilarated. The night might not have gone as she expected—and what had she expected, really?—but just when she needed something to happen in her life, just when she needed a little boost of something magical, she'd kissed that gorgeous man senseless to the point that he'd passed out. She'd like to look at it that way.

She grinned, remembering how her hands and mouth had explored his body. She'd had a night to remember, one for her diary.

When she got home and brewed a pot of coffee and then headed into the bathroom for a hot shower, she couldn't stop thinking of Felix Sanchez. All he'd said. The way he'd kissed her. Touched her. Looked at her, up and down, down and up. The way he'd told her the truth. *I'm not ready...*

Yes, one for the diary. Then she'd try her best to forget about Felix, even though she knew that would take a good long while.

Chapter Three

Felix needed coffee and a lot of it. And something for his headache. He stopped in his en suite bathroom for some acetaminophen, the cold water to swallow the tablets soothing his parched throat.

The house was hardly silent; his brothers had clearly come by, which made him wonder if Shari had hustled past them unseen. They were downstairs, talking about pancakes, the rodeo and major league baseball. His parents usually woke up around 7:30 a.m. His mother didn't have to be at the hair salon she owned till ten, and his dad, a postal worker, was off on Fridays. His father and Stanley always spent Fridays together, tinkering on a project in the garage and then going out to lunch at their favorite eatery—the Gemstone Diner for the combo platters with a ton of fries in gravy.

He headed downstairs and found Dante and Dylan in the kitchen, both sipping coffee from mugs and arguing over the post season. Each was so determined to be right about their favorite teams that they barely paused to greet Felix, which let him know they *hadn't* seen Shari. *Phew.* He did not want to be questioned.

He was just pouring his coffee when his parents came downstairs, both in the matching plush white spa robes that his sister Sofia had bought them for Christmas last year. She gave each of her three sons a kiss.

"Where's Tío?" Denise Sanchez asked, her warm, dark eyes peering at Felix closely. She glanced across the hallway at the sliding glass doors to the patio, where Stanley liked to have his morning cafe con leche after his calisthenics. No Stanley out there.

"Wait a minute," his mother added, turning back to him. "Why do you look like you're ill? Are you feeling okay?" She reached up on tiptoe and laid the back of her hand on his forehead. "Hmm, you don't feel warm."

"I'm fine," he said. "Coffee, Dad?" he asked

his father to get the focus off him and his clearly hungover state.

"Definitely," Aaron Sanchez said. He leaned his ear up. "Why don't I hear Stanley singing or humming? He's still asleep? At this hour?"

Stanley was a notorious early riser. Six o'clock every morning for exercise on the patio, then after breakfast with the family he'd take a walk around the neighborhood, listening to his podcasts or mariachi music on the AirPods Felix had given him as a welcome gift.

Felix pretended not to hear the question as he poured cream and added a teaspoon of sugar into his coffee. He sipped. Ahh. He needed that. Between the steam and the caffeine, he felt himself coming back to life.

"Felix? Where's Stanley?" his mother asked again, sitting down at the table with her coffee.

"Maybe out for a drive?" Felix said. That wasn't a fib. His uncle *could* be out for a drive—coming back from Winona's place.

"Which one of you ate the last of the churros?" she asked, sitting down and taking a sip of her coffee. She raised an eyebrow and Dante and Dylan.

"Don't look at us," Dylan said.

Dante nodded. "But we would have eaten them if there had been any."

"That was definitely Tio," he said.

There. Maybe his mother would be so mad at Stanley that she wouldn't care where he was. Because Felix wasn't about to reveal that Stanley Sanchez had met a woman and left the bar with her last night. And was still out.

A key could be heard in the lock.

"Ah, that must be him," his father said, taking another sip of his coffee and rooting around in the fridge. "Who wants pancakes? Chocolate chip? Side of bacon?"

"Definitely me," Dante said.

Dylan grinned. "Ditto."

"Make a stack of both for me," Felix said, getting up to pour himself another mug of coffee. He needed more caffeine and lots of carbs—stat. "And thanks."

Stanley was singing a Frank Sinatra song as he appeared in the doorway. "I've Got You Under My Skin." His great-uncle didn't listen to Frank Sinatra. But he clearly had last night.

"How was your walk?" Aaron asked his uncle.

"My walk?" Stanley repeated.

"Weren't you out on your morning walk?" Denise asked.

Stanley grinned a bit sheepishly. "Well, if you must know, no. I was at the home of a new lady friend." He did a little cha-cha dance, then walked over to the coffeepot and poured a mug of coffee.

"I met someone special last night. Didn't Felix tell you?"

His parents and brothers all stared at Felix, then at Stanley as he sat down. "I didn't want to talk behind your back."

"Talk away!" Stanley said. "You might have told your *mami* and *papi* about Winona's lovely white hair, how it glistens in the moonlight."

His parents' eyes widened as they looked at each other, then at Felix then back at Stanley.

"Winona?" his mother repeated. "The only Winona I know in Bronco is Winona Cobbs. The psychic."

"The very lovely lady herself," Stanley said, a smile splitting his face. "A vision in purple. She told me she sees wonderful things for me in my future."

"Oh, did she?" Denise asked with a smile.

Aaron set down a big plate of pancakes and another of bacon. Felix's stomach growled and he grabbed a slice of bacon, then added three pancakes to his plate. His dad brought over the syrup and powdered sugar. He was grateful his father was doing all the work because Felix wasn't quite ready to stand and help with anything.

"Isn't Winona in her nineties?" Aaron asked. "An older woman?" He smiled, wiggling his eyebrows.

"My Celia was two years older," Stanley noted, taking a slice of bacon.

"So when are you seeing your lady friend again?" Dylan asked, also wiggling his eyebrows.

"For dinner tonight," Stanley said, his dark eyes twinkling. "Thank goodness we went out to Doug's last night, eh, Felix? I would have missed out on meeting her."

And I wouldn't have been sitting next to Shari Lormand at the bar, sharing her wings, and then kissing her in this very kitchen last night. Feeling her against me in bed. He would never forget the sight of her in her white bra and undies, her lush curves, that gorgeous strawberry blond hair, which he'd run his hands through all he'd wanted.

Well, until he'd fallen asleep.

And thank God he had. Because if he'd slept with her, he'd feel worse than he already did this morning. There couldn't be anything between them. Felix just wasn't ready for a relationship and wasn't sure when he would be. And because he'd practically seen her naked and her hand had been wrapped around certain hard parts of his body, having a casual friendship would seem…difficult.

But what to do this morning? He wouldn't pretend last night—and this morning—hadn't happened. He'd drop off a note with something from the bakery at the front desk of the library. Just to clear the air and they could both go on with their lives, the scone or pastry taking away any residual awkwardness. The library was right in the middle of downtown Bronco Heights, not far from the animal clinic where he'd be starting off his day, so yes, he'd drop that off during his lunch break.

And try to forget Shari, even though she'd been fully on his mind since he'd woken up.

"Can you help me find a book about a hamster that talks?"

Shari looked up from her desk in the Bronco Library's Children's Room at the cute little blond boy standing beside a tall woman. He couldn't be older than four.

"Don't forget to say 'excuse me' first," the woman said to him with a gentle smile.

"Excuse me," the boy said.

"Let's see," she said, typing into her search engine. "Ah, I've got a few picture books that you might like." She stood up and led the way to the shelves, plucking out the three books. *Henry Hamster Goes to Preschool, Harry Hamster Loves Vegetables*, and *I'm a Hamster, Not a Gerbil!* She handed the boy the colorful hardcover books, and he grinned and said, "Thanks!" and then ran over to the couch along the window.

She'd been busy all morning, a good thing.

Not much time to think about last night or this morning. Had it just been five hours ago that she'd woken up in Felix Sanchez's bed in her rumpled dress? She'd had a bowl of cereal and two cups of coffee so far, but what she really needed was a nap. With two story hours this morning, plus a bunch of ordering to do from the winter publishing catalogs, Shari wouldn't have a minute to herself until lunch. Again, probably a good thing. The more distance put between her and the memory of Felix, the more it would seem like a dream that couldn't possibly have happened.

Except it had happened. Her friend Evy had texted earlier this morning with a Well??? Anything happen between you Felix after driving him home last night? Shari had glanced around the bar for Evy last night so she could wave goodbye, and Evy had watched her and Felix leave with an excited look on her face. Shari had texted back a quick Let's talk tomorrow. Her friend had texted a few hours later with Sooo? and Shari had sent her a I'll fill you in after story time, which got her back an Oooh, can't wait!

At noon, Shari led the preschool-age story time in the fenced-in garden amid the fresh air and flowers and the interested, curious, happy faces in a semicircle around her, their parents and caregivers sitting on benches just a few feet away. Evy's four-year-old daughter, Lola, was in the group, Evy chatting with two other moms, each sipping from the complimentary coffee the library provided. Shari looked at each and every little face in the semicircle, their rapt attention, their impossibly soft cheeks.

Eye on the prize, she told herself. *Keep focused on what you want, not on what you want and can't have, such as Felix Sanchez. You made that mistake before and it was very painful.* As she'd told him last night when he'd told her he wasn't ready, she would not ignore a man telling her outright that he couldn't give her what she wanted. And what Shari Lormand wanted was marriage and family. If she couldn't have the marriage—at thirty-four and single it was looking less and less likely—she would create her own family.

Since her lunch break began when story time ended, she walked Evy and Lola into the Children's Room, and when Lola sat at a table to color with a friend, Evy grabbed her arm.

"Something happened!" she whispered, her pretty face very excited at the possibility. She whipped her long, dark ponytail behind her shoulder. "Tell me everything."

Shari smiled. "Well, there is actually something to tell."

"I knew it!" Evy said. "I saw that chemistry between you two."

Shari whispered the entire story, start to finish.

"Wow," Evy said. "You two really opened up to each other."

They had, unexpectedly and however briefly—in his kitchen.

"If only it could go somewhere," Shari said. "But he made it clear it can't. And I want what I want, so it can't for me, either."

"*Something* is going to happen next," Evy said. "I know it."

Shari shook her head. "Nope. I will not hear from him again. And I will certainly not chase after someone who told me loud and clear that he's not looking for a relationship."

"I wouldn't give up on the man so fast," Evy said. "As I learned with Wes, what a guy insists and what he feels can be two different things until he's knocked upside the head with how in love he is."

Shari laughed. "Well, I don't think anyone's in love—except you and Wes."

The front desk librarian walked in holding a take-out cup of coffee and a small box from Bronco Java and Juice, one of Shari's favorite places to unwind with a book on her lunch break. "Special delivery for Shari."

"For me?" Shari asked.

"Very good-looking guy dropped it off just a minute ago. Enjoy," she added, setting the coffee and the box on the table and heading back out. There was a little card taped to the box.

Shari's mouth almost dropped open.

"Well, I have one guess who that very good-looking man was," Evy said with a grin. "Open the card!"

Shari grinned back and grabbed the small card with illustrated flowers.

Thank you again for the ride home, Shari. All best, Felix Sanchez.

Shari's heart plummeted.

Even Evy looked deflated. "He did *not* write All Best," she said, shaking her head.

"Yup. And we know what that means. 'Thanks and see you around town if we happen to run into each other, which we won't because you don't have pets and I don't have kids so no chance of that. Have a nice life!'"

"But," Evy said. "But! He *did* think of you this morning. He did go to Bronco Java and Juice and buy you a coffee and whatever is in that box."

Shari opened the box and found three churros inside. Her heart gave a little leap. A wary leap, but still. "Hmm," she said. "Now, if there had been a scone in there or a Danish or a donut, I wouldn't read anything into it. But churros. Java and Juice has them only every Friday morning so Felix clearly went there especially to get them for you."

When she'd whispered the story of last night and this morning to Evy, Shari had not left out the churros as what had gotten her to accept Felix's offer to come into his house for a bit. Or how there had only been crumbs.

"I so agree," Evy said with a grin. "He's making up for something here. You have not seen the last of the guy."

"Wait. Is that a good thing, though? I can't get hung up on a man who's not ready to be in a relationship. I'm thirty-four. I want a child. I want a family." She bit her lip and shook her head. "No, I'm definitely not going to do this—get all wrapped up in a man who can't give me what I want. It's the definition of dopey."

Evy tilted her head. "I'm just saying that I didn't think Wes would come around to opening up that guarded heart of his to a single mother and child. But he did."

Felix's gorgeous face floated into her mind. The sweet stories he'd told her about his family. His furry patients. *No, no, no*, she told herself. *Do not get roped in by that face and how much you like him! Do. Not.*

"Okay, here's how you know if you should stop

by the clinic to thank him for the coffee and chur-ros," Evy said.

Shari raised an eyebrow.

"Taste the coffee to see what it is," Evy said. "If it's a latte or an Americano, he's more open to get-ting involved than he knows since he put thought and a little something extra into it. If it's just a plain old coffee, then maybe he's just being nice."

Shari stared at the coffee. She could detect a hint of sweetness coming from the tiny spout in the lid. She lifted the cup to her lips and took a sip. "Oh, my," she said.

"What is it?" Evy asked, eyes dying to know.

"A mocha latte with whipped cream." She took another sip, the hot, sweet creamy brew going straight to her heart.

Evy gave a little clap. "I have a feeling your nights are gonna get busy, Shari."

The problem was she wanted to hope so, and yet she still told herself she couldn't set herself up for heartbreak again. No, her nights would not get busy.

"Besides, you'll need a plus-one for the grand opening of Cimarron Rose," Evy added.

"I can't wait to see what you've done with the space." Evy was so young, just twenty-five, but she'd had big dreams to open up her own boutique and she had. Cimarron Rose was a boho-meets-cowgirl shop in Bronco Valley and would sell clothing and accessories and some home goods. Shari couldn't wait for the grand opening to buy a few things to support her friend.

She took another sip of her delicious mocha latte. "Well, I'll definitely be there. Solo."

"Even if you don't invite him, he'll be getting an invitation. So you definitely will see him again." Evy wiggled her eyebrows.

Shari gave an inward sigh. "I have to let him go. Not that I ever had him. I have to get him out of my head. I have to remember what I want. A family."

Evy squeezed her hand. "Just be open to everything, then. Including unforeseen possibilities with Felix Sanchez. The mocha latte doesn't lie," she added with a joyful grin.

Shari stared at the cup, the box of churros beside it. She took another sip of the latte. Definitely an order with thought put into it. Nothing quick like regular old coffee and a bagel with cream cheese.

Shari was clearly too hopeful if she was banking on a coffee drink predicting her future.

Maybe what she needed was to make an appointment with the town psychic, Winona Cobbs, who suddenly had a special insight into the name Sanchez.

Yes, Shari thought. *I'll do just that.*

Chapter Four

After giving his last patient of the day at the clinic a treat and a good scratch behind his ears, Felix hung up his white lab coat and headed out of the exam room. He was surprised to find his uncle Stanley sitting in the waiting area in front of the huge fish tank. His uncle wore his favorite outfit of jeans, a Western shirt with silver snaps, and a leather vest over it along with a black cowboy hat on his head. His belt buckle had the etching of the Mexican flag.

Felix waved goodbye to the receptionist, who would be closing up in a half hour. "I'm glad you're here, Tio," he said as they walked out into the beautiful mid-September evening, low sixties with a nice breeze. "We didn't get to talk earlier since I had to get to the clinic, but I'd love to hear about your night."

"And I'd love to hear how *you* got home last night," Stanley said with a prompting smile. "Winona and I were at Lookout Point when I realized I'd stranded you without the car keys. Know what she said?"

Ha—so Felix had been right. The senior love-birds had been at Lookout Point and his uncle probably had been singing Winona mariachi songs. But his date clearly hadn't run for the hills. "What did she say?"

"She said, 'Oh, no worries, Stanley. That lovely gal sitting next to Felix will take care of him tonight.'"

Felix almost gasped. "She said that?"

Stanley grinned, then let out a hoot of laughter. "Yes, she did. And did that lovely gal take care of you last night?"

Felix swallowed. Just how gifted a psychic was Winona?

"She gave me a ride home and came in for a bit," Felix said. A bit *overnight*, but he wasn't going to mention that.

Stanley rubbed his hands together. "Oh, did she, now?"

"Tio, listen. Shari and I will just be friends. I'm not looking to get involved with anyone. I'm just not ready."

"I didn't think I was ready," Stanley said as they reached the parking lot. "I've met so many nice women since I've been in Montana. I mistook *not ready* for the earth not shaking."

Felix raised an eyebrow. "The earth shook last night?"

Stanley smiled. "Did I *leave* Doug's with Winona? Was I out *all night*? The earth shook. And then we made it shake." He laughed, then said, "Actually, we didn't. We did kiss, though. Quite a bit. And danced at Lookout Point and at Winona's house. She lives with her daughter Dorothea and granddaughter, Wanda. I slept on the couch. We're having a repeat tonight."

Felix looked closely at Stanley and could see happiness radiating from the man. "I'm glad, Tio. I really am. But, again, I'm not ready."

The earth did shake for Felix last night, though. Or else he wouldn't have even wanted to *kiss* Shari. Since his loss, he'd never reacted to a woman like that.

"Did you send her flowers for driving you home because of me?" Stanley asked.

"Coffee and churros, actually," he said.

"Ah, so the earth *did* move," Stanley insisted. "Otherwise you would have let it go."

Felix thought about that for a moment. Maybe. But the ride home seemed to warrant a proper thank-you. And given that things got very personal, he'd wanted to make the thank-you a bit more personal. But that was exactly why he'd added *All best, Felix* to the little card attached to the box. And when she'd sent a text not long after he'd dropped off the coffee and churros— just a short and simple Thank you for the treats... delicious!—he wrote back with Glad you enjoyed them. All best, Felix.

He'd specifically jotted All best, Felix both times because he needed that bit of professionalism. Something he'd write to a client.

Something that didn't leave any doors open. In fact, that *shut* any doors. He wasn't open to a relationship, and Shari wanted a serious relationship, leading to a husband and children. He couldn't be that guy.

So he had no business letting their association continue beyond their two short and sweet communications. He'd achieved his goal; the gift had worked, she'd responded just right. He could move on with his evening...and his life.

But once again, he couldn't get her out of his

mind. And the yearning to see her was something new. Something scary.

"Felix!" a familiar female voice called out.

He turned around. And there was Shari Lormand running toward him, her strawberry blond hair flying behind her. She wore a multicolored tweed blazer over a long dress and had on a different interesting necklace today and many wooden bracelets.

She was also carrying a small cardboard box with care. "I'm so relieved I caught you!" she said. "I had an evening youth event with the middle schoolers at the library, and we found a tiny kitten all alone in the garden. She was in a recessed area near the wrought-iron fence." She held out the box for him to see.

He peered in. A kitten, no more than three months old, looked up at him with slightly watery eyes. She'd need attention right away.

"I will leave you to care for your new patient," Stanley said, looking at Shari eagerly.

Oh, I'm sure you will, Felix thought. "Stanley Sanchez, this is Shari Lormand. Shari, my uncle Stanley."

Stanley gave her arm a warm pat. "Thank you for rescuing my nephew last night. And now you are rescuing this sweet *gatita*."

"It was my pleasure to do both," Shari said.

Felix smiled. "Well, let's take the kitty in and assess her."

"I'll see you later, Feel," Stanley said and then hurried to his truck.

"I wasn't sure if I should bring him here or to the animal shelter," Shari said, "but your office was closer, so I ran over."

"You did the right thing," he said. He took the box from her, and he could see the relief on her face that the little kitten would be taken care of. Shari Lormand was definitely a woman who cared.

He held open the door to the clinic and went in after her. "New patient," he said to the receptionist, Allie. "I'll type up the notes, so feel free to head out for the day."

Allie came over to peer in the box. "Aww. Hope the kitty will be okay."

"Might be a stray who got separated from her mama and the litter," Felix said. "She looks sturdy enough."

Felix held open the door to Exam Room 1 and followed Shari in. "Sure is cute," he said, taking out the gray, white and black kitten and examining her in his hands. "No wounds. That's a good thing." He grabbed the padded basket from the table behind him and set the kitten inside to do a more comprehensive exam.

A half hour later, the kitten was resting in the

basket after receiving vaccinations and treatment for ear mites, along with some food and water.

"I'll need to find a foster home for her at least tonight since the shelter is closed now," he said, gently petting the kitten's back. "And I'll check the library garden and surrounding areas for the mother cat and any other stray kittens."

"Well, I could foster her for the weekend since I'll be home anyway."

That was kind of her. Kind of her to bring in the kitten and offer the weekend home. "Perfect," he said. "Bring her back here Monday and I'll take her over to the animal shelter. They'll have plenty of foster homes available while she gets in tip-top shape for adoption."

"I've never taken care of a kitten before," she said. "What should I pick up to have at home?"

"I've got a kitten starter pack, actually. The clinic gets a lot of freebies that companies hope will get good reviews and word of mouth. It has food and water dishes, a kitten-sized litter box and fine clay litter. A bag of food and toys. And I can give you a kitten carrier to transport her home in. She'll be feeling so much better within a half hour from just the treatments and food and hydration that she'd probably go leaping out of that little box you brought her in."

"Glad to hear it," she said, giving the kitty a

scratch under her chin. The kitten rubbed against Shari's hand. "Should we name her? Or let the shelter do that?"

"You've got naming rights."

Shari tilted her head and regarded the kitten. "I think we have to name her Page since she was found at the library."

He smiled. "A literary kitty. I'll just go get that starter pack and the carrier. Back in a flash."

Anyone who loved animals, who'd rush an ailing kitten to a vet's clinic, was all right in Felix's book. It occurred to him that they could be friends. Who couldn't use a new friend? Someone easy to talk to. He didn't have many women friends or even acquaintances since his and Victoria's former "circle" had slowly distanced himself from him. People got uncomfortable with cancer. With death. With how to include the new widower in the old group. Dynamics had changed and Felix found himself getting fewer and fewer invitations. Of course, that had been fine with him. He wasn't much for dinner parties anyway. But it had felt good to open up to Shari last night. He hadn't done that outside of his family in a long time.

Friends. He nodded to himself as he headed down to the hall to the supplies closet. With a label, he wouldn't even have to think about his attraction to Shari; he simply wouldn't act on it. Because they were friends.

The starter pack bag in one hand and the carrier in the other, he went back to the exam room. Shari was holding the kitten in her lap on the floor, telling Page that she didn't know anything about kittens or cats, but she'd give her a good weekend home, she promised.

"I see a foster fail in your future," he said with a grin.

"I don't know. I probably will get too attached, but I don't like the idea of leaving a young kitten home alone for eight hours while I'm at work." She picked up Page and held her high, giving her a kiss on the nose. "Though you are seriously cute."

Felix set the carrier on the exam table, put a folded blanket inside, and then took the kitten from Shari and put her inside, zipping up the soft opening. "At three months, she'd be fine on her own and would probably nap a good portion of the day. But there are plenty of people looking to foster or adopt kittens, so no worries either way."

He could tell she was already too smitten with the tiny bundle of fur.

"Ready, Page?" She picked up the carrier and held it up so she could see the kitty and assure her.

Oh, yeah. Foster fail was coming.

"So I'll help you get all this stuff home," Felix

said, "and then I'll go look for the mother cat and other kittens."

"I live just two blocks from here. You know the condos on Oak Street?"

He nodded. "My brothers looked at a place there when they were looking to move out. They almost rented in BH247—you know, that swanky complex geared to singles? But they opted to stay in Bronco Valley."

"I looked at that complex when I first moved here, but it seemed a little too 'singles scene' for me," she said. "That was back when I was freshly heartbroken, though. A coworker who lives there met her fiancé at the pool. She keeps telling me to move there and I'd be married within six months. I've been considering it lately, too."

A good reminder that Shari Lormand was looking to get married. And that for him, she was strictly in the friend zone. She wanted a life that he was unwilling to give her.

"Ready to go, *amiga*?" he asked, trying out the word on his tongue. It felt…forced.

"Ready," she said.

Ready to be friends. Ready to let Shari into his life under this new parameter. But could you be friends with a woman you couldn't help noticing little things about? Like the way the light from the setting sun lit up her beautiful hair. Like the way her little tweed blazer highlighted her curves. Like how beautiful she was. Inside and out.

Could you be friends with a woman you wanted to kiss right now?

Last night, Shari was at Felix's place. Tonight, he was at her place. How did this keep happening? He'd helped her home with the kitten and the starter pack, then had left to search for the mother cat in the library garden and vicinity.

"Maybe you're my good luck charm," she said to Page, who was exploring the corner of the living room where Felix had set her padded basket, which would double as her bed. Shari had a few baskets and could put one in each room. She had her food and water dishes on a little mat in the kitchen, and the litter box was in the bathroom, which was thankfully large. A few catnip toys and two plastic hollow balls were on the rug, but right now Page was more interested in the empty shoe box Felix had told her would be kitten heaven. Page kept jumping in, going on her back, kicking at the sides, crouching down, and then catapulting herself out of it, then running back inside. Now she was licking her paw and grooming her face.

Shari had thought a lot about what Evy said, that she shouldn't give up on Felix so fast. As if she could. This was the guy she'd had her first crush on. Instead of guarding her heart, she was hopeful. And she wasn't sure that was a good plan of action.

And her plan of action was important. If she wanted to make her most fervent dream come true, to have a family of her own, she had to work toward that, not against it. And working toward it meant only being attracted to emotionally available men. Not men who straight out told her they weren't looking for a relationship.

A half hour later, Felix knocked on her door.

"No sign of the mother cat or any other kittens. Page must have gotten separated at some point. I'm really glad you found her."

"Me, too," she said. "And thank you for examining her. I like knowing she's on the mend."

"Well, I'll head home, then," he said. "Unless you have any questions about fostering or kitten care. I know it's just the weekend, but better to be in the know."

"Actually, I have a lot of questions, but I didn't want to keep you. I'm a total newbie at this. I can trade you tips for pesto pasta and garlic bread. The pesto isn't homemade, but it's still scrumptious."

Shari, Shari, Shari, she mentally chastised herself. *What do you think you're doing? How did you go from trying to get Felix Sanchez out of your head to inviting him in for a home-cooked meal?*

"You don't have to go to all that trouble of making dinner," he said. "I'm happy to offer advice."

"No trouble at all," she heard herself say, despite how untrue it was. It was trouble for her as a woman who was going to get hurt again. "And honestly, because I've never had a cat before, let alone a baby cat, I'd feel better having you here to make sure all is well before I officially take over." That part was actually true.

He looked around the living room. "House-proofing wise, just move that pot of African violets from the windowsill to where Page couldn't possibly get to it. Several plants and flowers are poisonous to cats. And avoid giving her people food. The kitten chow is good for right now. And no milk—it can actually cause belly trouble."

Huh. Now she was a little glad she'd invited him to stay for dinner. "Got it," she said. "No saucers of milk even though I always see that in movies." She walked over to the window and grabbed the African violet and set it on the top of the refrigerator for now. She was not only attached to Felix Sanchez, she was attached to that tiny ball of gray, black and white fur running around the living room, knocking around her little catnip mouse.

Get your head on straight, she told herself, hurrying into the kitchen. She rooted around the cupboards and pulled out what she needed.

"Can I help?" he asked, standing in the doorway. More like *filling* the doorway with his broad shoulders. For a moment she couldn't drag her eyes off him.

"Your job can be just keeping an eye on Page," she said. "I've got this."

He smiled and headed into the living room.

As she waited for the pasta to boil and the sauce to heat, she could hear Felix talking to the kitten. "Now, just because you're adorable doesn't mean you get to pee wherever you want, Page. There are rules when you live in a warm, cozy home like this. We showed you where the litter box is, remember? Good. And don't think that super cute face or the black smudge on your nose will get you out of trouble if you use those nails on Shari's nice red sofa. Use your new scratching post only. Got it, furball?"

Shari grinned. She would not be surprised if the kitten meowed a *yes*.

"I appreciate you giving her the house rules," she called out. What she didn't appreciate was how she was liking him more and more every minute.

She sighed as she drained the pasta and poured it into the fragrant pan with the pesto sauce. She gave it a good stir, then took the garlic bread from the oven.

"Something smells amazing," he called back.

"And it's ready, too," she said. She put the pasta in a serving dish and the bread in a lined basket and set everything on the kitchen table. She was itching to light the pretty candlesticks that her co-workers at the library had given her for Christmas last year, but as she well knew, this was not a date.

"Wow," he said as he sat down. "Looks as amazing as it smells." He heaped pasta on his plate and took a piece of garlic bread. "So I've been thinking."

"Oh?" She sat up straight.

That there was something so special between them he wanted to explore dating. Just give it a try. Because he could not stop thinking about her. And their almost evening together.

Yes, say all that, Felix Sanchez, she thought, trying to appear nonchalant as she scooped pasta on her plate.

"I want to be honest with you, Shari. Very honest. I did have a little too much to drink last night and the sangria on top of it, and I guess a part of me deep down wants what it wants. But in the cold light of day, I know I'm not ready to start dating. Or interested in dating. But I sense that you're a special person, Shari Lormand, and I'm so comfortable with you. Around you. I can talk to you." He took a sip of his white wine. "The fact that I'm saying any of this is a testament to that."

She ate a forkful of linguini pesto to seem as if she wasn't hanging on every word, waiting for the finale. She wasn't sure where he was headed with this. But every cell in her body was on alert.

"So I have a proposal for you."

A proposal, a proposal, a proposal. From not ready to date to a proposal. She could hear the sad trombone playing in her head. Surely this wasn't going anywhere good.

He held up his glass of wine. "I'd really like for us to be friends, Shari. And I don't mean acquaintances who run into each other occasionally and maybe have coffee every six months. I mean real friends. You feel down in the dumps, you call me and we go to the movies. I have a long, rough day and need some cheering up? I call you and we go to Bronco Brick Oven Pizza and you tell me some good jokes."

Friends. Real friends. She wondered if he could see how deflated she'd gotten, from sitting up straight, ears perked up to kind of slumped in her chair. Friends.

Who couldn't use a good friend? she thought, twirling the linguini around her fork. Friends were everything. Friends got you through. She'd just have to adjust her mindset about Felix Sanchez, not see him as anything more. But how did you go about doing that? How could you have a great time with your buddy eating pineapple pizza and seeing the new Marvel movie when you were so physically attracted to that buddy that you couldn't stop imaging the two of you in bed. Where you'd briefly been.

Then again, maybe she could handle a friendship with him. She'd just have to take it day by day.

Okay. Friends.

She ate her pasta, trying to think of a joke. Something to start their friendship off. "Do you like book humor?" she asked. "That's all I've got."

"Hit me," he said with a smile—that honestly stole her breath for a second.

"How do books stay warm in the winter?" she asked. "They wear book jackets. Badumpa!"

He had the decency to laugh because he was a great guy. "That's the kind of goofy joke I need after a rough day with a dog fighting for its life or a sick baby goat."

Oh, Felix. Yes, I want to be your friend. Much more. But yes.

"Then I'm the friend for you," she said lightly, but she felt anything but light. Or happy. Could they really be friends? When she wanted to rip his clothes off and feel the weight of him on top of her? When she wanted to kiss him with all the passion pent up inside her?

She really didn't know. The more she'd get to

know him, the harder she'd fall for him. And one day she'd be hanging out with him and her heart would ache and she'd know she'd fallen deeply in love with her...buddy.

She tried to remember Evy's advice. *Don't give up on him.* Maybe this was all part of the slow steps toward the two of them being more? Hmm, she thought as she ate another bite of pasta. That was possible. Entirely possible.

"Hit me with another book joke," he said.

She took a piece of bread from the basket and ate a deliciously buttery, garlicky piece. When you didn't have to worry about garlic breath because you would *not* be kissing afterward, you could really enjoy dinner that much more. A plus, she told herself. There was a silver lining to being friends with Felix. "Okay, I've got one," she said. "Why was the math textbook so sad?"

He tilted his head and paused with his linguini-laden fork midair. "Why?"

"Because it had so many problems."

He laughed again, his hazel eyes twinkling and tender, and raised his glass. "To being friends?"

She lifted hers. She hesitated on the clink, though. But she finally did. "To being friends," she repeated.

"Good," he said, his smile lighting up that handsome face that she wanted to kiss so badly.

Here's more library humor, she thought, biting into another piece of supposed silver-lining garlic bread. *Why was the librarian crying? Because she wrote the book on heartache yet chose to be buddies with a man she was in love with.*

Now that was no laughing matter.

He could *fall madly in love with you*, she reminded herself. *He does seem to really like your hair, for one. And your jokes. And you do talk easily. And he wants you. You know he does, even if he's going to suppress the attraction with all his might.*

Patience, she told herself, perking herself up, then felt something on her leg.

She looked down and there was Page, her front paws on Shari's shin.

"No linguini pesto for you," she said to the kitten. "But I'll play catch the catnip mouse with you after dinner." Page let out a pitiful meow. "Okay, fine. You can sit on my lap." She scooped up the sweet bundle of fur and settled her on her lap.

Felix grinned. "Yeah, you won't be giving up that kitten anytime soon."

She did like the idea of having a cute little someone to come home to. To tell her troubles to. And since she couldn't share her fears about Felix the friend *with* Felix the friend, Page was going to be her new nightly confidante.

Chapter Five

Anytime Felix was due for a haircut, he liked to make an appointment at his mother's salon in Bronco Valley instead of letting her snip away in the bathroom of their house with a towel over his shoulders like she used to do with all the Sanchez kids when they were younger. A home haircut meant an endless barrage of questions about his personal life while he was trapped beneath her scissors, brush and piercing gaze. At the salon, where she was the ultimate professional and surrounded by other stylists and customers, he knew he'd get a great haircut and few personal questions.

Now, after a morning making ranch calls, he'd

wolfed down a quick lunch in his SUV, and then headed to his mother's salon. He said several hellos to the other stylists and customers, smiled, answered questions, including two about dogs, then finally settled himself in the big chair, his mother draping a silver smock around him. He was glad he'd been so busy all morning and now was here because it had left no time to check in with Shari on how her first night as a foster kitty mom had gone.

Now that they were friends and had that distancing label between them, he shouldn't have a problem texting or stopping by the library—but he did. He'd been awake for a while last night thinking about her, unable to fall asleep, her pretty face and gorgeous strawberry blond hair, and how she'd looked in her white cotton bra and underwear in his bedroom, and he wasn't so quick to go see her. Maybe a few days of not seeing her would tamp down his attraction. But he doubted it.

"So, Felix," Denise Sanchez began, not catching his eye in the big round mirror in front of him, which told him she was up to no good. "I mentioned to one of my best clients that you were probably looking for a date for your cousin's quinceañera Friday night, and she got very excited about giving me her daughter's number. She's a busy lawyer, smart as can be and very pretty. I've seen a recent photo."

Because she was his mother, she thought nothing of tucking the slip of paper into the back pocket of his pants. "There. Now you have it." She started snipping, suddenly humming a song all innocent-like.

He'd forgotten about his cousin's quinceañera. A traditional celebration for girls turning fifteen, the party would be elaborate, festive and long. His cousins had rented out a venue that generally held weddings and over two hundred people were expected. Many would be loud teenagers.

Snip, snip, snip. "She's expecting your call, Felix. No later than end of business today, okay, *mijo*?" This time she did look at him in the mirror. Snip, snip-snip.

"Mom, first of all, you should have asked me before telling anyone I'd call their daughter for a date. Second, I..." *Think fast, Felix.* A good excuse that would shut her down from the subject. He'd used every one in the book the last couple of years. All he'd gotten from his mother was narrowed eyes, hands on hips, and a *Felix, I just want you to be happy*.

"She's thirty and marriage minded, of course," his mother continued. "And she's allergic to dogs but she's fine with cats."

"Mom, you'll have to tell your client that you were mistaken about me looking for a date."

Denise moved to the other side of the chair and snipped away. "It's just one date, Felix. So unless you already *have* a date, I can't lie to my best client."

There it was. The excuse he hadn't used yet. "I do already have a date, actually."

His mother paused midsnip, her brown eyes lighting up. "You do?"

Shari Lormand's face floated into his mind. "Yes. Her name is Shari. She's a librarian. Children's department. So I can't possibly call your client's daughter."

Denise Sanchez's hand flew to her heart, and she waved at her face with the other. "A children's librarian! She must *love* kids. She sounds wonderful! Oh, I'm so excited to meet her."

His mother sure was predictable. He loved her, but boy, did he have her number.

Hopefully, his newly named buddy was free Friday night.

"You like this Shari?" his mother asked, turning his chair slightly to the left. He wished she hadn't done that because now he realized that both the stylist and customer in the chair just a few feet away were listening to every word and awaiting his answer.

"She's a really good person," he said.

"Pretty?"

"Yes, Mom. She's pretty."

"Marriage minded?"

The stylist to his left began pointing a piece of tin foil in their direction. Her customer had foils folded all over her head in a pyramid shape. "You can't be too sure these days, so it's a good question. My daughter is twenty-nine and keeps saying she's focusing on herself and her career. Her career is not going to keep her company. Her career is not going to bring her chicken soup when she's sick. Her career is not going to give me grandbabies!"

Denise Sanchez did an exaggerated nod. "Is Shari in her twenties? Or thirties?"

"Mom, Shari's age and how she conducts her life is her concern. Not mine or anyone else's."

"Until you want to start a family and she's busy with her career!" the stylist said. Her customer gave a firm nod.

"Well, if I did get married someday way in the future and my wife and I did have a baby," Felix said, "maybe I would be the one to stay home so that my wife could focus on her career."

"Huh," Denise said. "I suppose so. Things are different than when I got married." Nods from the other stylist and her customer. She waved her hand in the air. "Well, you and Shari will figure all that out."

Whoa. Wait just a minute. In the space of two minutes, Shari went from being his plus-one to a family party to the mother of his children.

"Mom, first of all, let's not get way ahead of ourselves. And second of all, you never stopped working. Yeah, a family of seven needed two paychecks, but your kids are all grown up. You love what you do and that's why you're cutting my hair right now."

"True. If we were rich Bronco Heights types, I'd still cut hair. It's my passion."

He smiled. "Exactly." He was grateful when she swiveled her chair back toward the center. Now it was time to get the focus off *his* love life. "So, Mom," he said, lowering his voice, "what do you think about Tio's new romance?"

"I think it's wonderful. Stanley lost the sparkle in his eye when Celia died, but now, it's back. And it's a good example for you, *mijo*."

He inwardly sighed.

"Felix, if Stanley could date again after sixty years of marriage to a woman he loved with all his heart and soul, so can you. I know your loss might still feel raw. But three years is a long time."

Why did he think getting his hair cut in the

salon would prevent personal conversation? This couldn't get more personal.

He stared at himself in the mirror, avoiding catching his mother's eye. He looked like the same Felix. But three years ago his life had completely changed and no matter how many times his family told him it was okay to get back out there, their voices full of compassion, he just wanted to put his hands over his ears and shut out their well-meaning words.

"I'm so glad you're bringing Shari to a big family party," his mother continued. "For you, that means you're serious. Oh, I can't wait to tell everyone."

Uh-oh.

"Mom, it's a date to a teenager's birthday party. A first step. That's all."

A first step, he saw her mouth with a gleam in her eye to the other stylist.

A first step into assuring him that he and Shari Lormand were meant to be friends and only friends.

"Thank you. See you then," Shari said into her phone, then put it down on the kitchen table—and let out a happy-scared squeal. "Page! Guess what?"

Page did not come running; the kitten was grooming herself on the sofa, not even looking

Shari's way, but hey, she was a living, breathing being to share her big news with.

"I made an appointment with a fertility clinic to discuss my options!" Shari announced.

After the "will you be my friend" conversation with Felix last night, Shari had woken up that morning determined to be proactive about her dreams and goals for a family. And she got lucky. It turned out there was a cancellation today at Big Sky Fertility Clinic—about thirty minutes away from Bronco—and Shari grabbed the 4:45 appointment. When she got out of work at four, she'd hurry home, feed and play with Page and then drive out to the clinic.

She'd couldn't put her life and dreams on hold for a man. Did she wish Felix was emotionally available? Yes. Did she wish they could pursue a romantic relationship? Yes. Would she hold her breath on either? No.

Did she now have butterflies flapping away in her belly? Oh, yes. She had so much nervous energy that she decided to just head to work a half hour early.

As the first employee to arrive at the library, she made a pot of coffee, wondering if soon she'd be making decaf for herself. She felt a happy chill run up her spine. Then a scared chill ran down.

As she took her coffee to her desk and turned on

her desktop, Shari pictured herself holding a baby.
Buying diapers at the grocery store. She wanted to
be a mother and today was the start of her dream.

The day went very slowly, of course. That was
always the case when she was watching the clock,
something she rarely did. With twenty minutes
left of her shift, she was looking through the winter catalogs from publishers for new books to
order when a woman she recognized as a waitress at the diner and her young daughter came up
to her desk. Ariel and her daughter, Mia, had the
same pretty fine blond hair and pale brown eyes.
Shari had overheard a few conversations between
waitresses while having breakfast or lunch at the
counter enough to know that Ariel's ex-husband
had abandoned her when Mia was just a baby.

"Excuse me, could you point me in the right
direction for books for my daughter?" Allison
asked. "She's six years old and in the first grade at
Bronco Elementary. Mia usually gets books from
her classroom or the school library but she acci-
dentally left her book on her desk."

"Why do I have to read at home when I read
at school?" Mia asked her mother on a pleading
whine. "I hate reading. I'm bad at it."

"Honey, Ms. Templeton said you should spend
twenty minutes on reading at home," Allison said

with a mixture of exhaustion and impatience in her voice. "Plus, we have to fill out your reading log."

Mia frowned and crossed her arms over her chest.

Shari gave Ariel an "I've got this" nod and leaned toward the girl. "Mia, tell me two things that you like. Really, really like."

Mia tilted her head. "I like French fries. And I like going really fast on the tire swings at recess."

"What if I told you that I could find two fun-to-read books about French fries and swinging on tire swings?" Shari asked. "Would you like to read those?"

The girl's brown eyes widened with interest—wary interest. "Yes!"

Shari tapped at the search engine. She found two cute books on those very topics with great illustrations that would capture the attention of a reluctant reader. Ariel smiled at Shari and then sank down gratefully on a sofa with an exhausted sigh.

Shari led the way over to the bookcase full of picture books and had the girl help her find the titles.

Mia thanked her and ran over to her mom, plopping down and opening one of the books. Shari watched her move her finger along the few lines of text on each page.

When Mia finished the book, Shari watched

her mother almost brace herself to get off the sofa, the fatigue in her eyes and body language visible. But every time her daughter looked at her, her face brightened and she spoke to Mia with energy.

This was what single motherhood would be like, Shari knew. Your heart running around the library, your child sliding a finger under the words she's struggling to read. And you've got everything heaped on your plate. It might be the weekend, but Mia's mother would go home and have to figure out dinner. Then in the morning it would be breakfast and planning the day and making lunch and tidying up the home. Then oversee homework due the next day and sign off on reading logs and go through folders of information. Another dinner to plan and make. More clean up. Then it would be work on Monday.

Sometimes when Shari saw firsthand even just a tidbit of how hard it was to be a single parent, she would put the thought of sperm donors and IVF or foster parenthood and adoption out of her mind, scared to even think more about those options. Parenthood was challenging enough with a loving spouse at your side.

But she was thirty-four and could not be more single. The only man she was interested in had friend zoned her last night.

How did you know when to give up on a

dream—marriage with a man she loved, who loved her, and a baby—if time for that baby was ticking away?

As Mia and her mom were leaving, she caught sight of Mia throwing her arms around her mother and hugging her with such love and devotion, Allison scooping her up for a hug and a little duet that must have been a thing they did. And just like that, Shari's heart was soothed and she knew she could do this—face motherhood on her own. Parenthood would be as rewarding as it was challenging.

I want a child, Shari thought again. She knew it with absolute certainty. So yes, she was scared. But she'd always known being a mother would require everything out of her, whether she had a loving, supportive partner or not.

At four, Shari left the library and went home, her bundle of fur yawning in her kitty bed and going right back to sleep. Shari gave her a gentle scratch on her cute head, filled up her dinner bowl and headed out.

The Big Sky Fertility Center looked so inviting. It was housed in a pale peach Victorian at the end of the main street in Wonderstone Ridge, a much bigger town than Bronco about thirty minutes north. Shari went in, taking a deep breath as she pulled open the inside door. The waiting room was crowded with all kinds of people, all kinds of couples.

And now that she was here, she felt so...alone. She tried to perk herself up, to remember how proactive she'd felt this morning when she'd made the appointment.

As she sat down, she realized she should have brought a friend. Someone who'd support her, hold her hand when need be, just be there. Someone like Evy, but Evy had way too much going on for Shari to feel comfortable asking her to take hours from her day to sit at her side, especially when she wasn't even sure this was the right path to motherhood.

And there was no way she could have asked Felix. This was way too personal, too complex, too everything for someone she'd only recently met, no matter how close to him she felt. Besides, if she planned to be a single parent by choice, she'd better get used to being on her own.

On my own. Exactly how I don't want to be.

She couldn't let the chance to have a baby or be a foster parent slip through her fingers.

Suddenly, she wished Felix were here beside her so she could talk all this through. Now that they were friends, maybe she *could* talk to him about this, get his point of view.

Her appointment was running twenty minutes late, so it was a good thing she wasn't expected back at the library. She picked up one of the brochures on the long coffee table and read through it. The information made everything sound less scary.

And the baby on the cover had Shari so wistful that she knew she was in the right place, that she was gathering facts, feeling things out, exploring her options.

An hour later, Shari had met with a fertility counselor, asked all her questions, had them answered, and put a mental check mark next to the idea of using an anonymous sperm donor. She would be able to choose her donor based on an in-depth profile. As she left, her head full of everything she'd learned, Shari knew she'd feel the same way about all the other options. All the paths to motherhood felt like real options for her. Right now, she was glad she *had* options and was finally starting on her journey.

Just as she stepped into the beautiful September late-afternoon breeze, her phone pinged with a text.

Felix.

Would you like to be my plus-one to a family birthday party Friday night? This is no ordinary teenage girl's party, though—it's a quinceañera and will be like a mini wedding in scale. Good food is guaranteed.

Her heart soared as if a teenaged Felix had asked her to the prom, not that that would have ever happened since he and Victoria had been a couple all four years of high school. But Shari wasn't a teenager with a crush anymore. She knew this wasn't a date. *It's why he very specifically referred to you as his plus one. It's what friends do.*

Still, she liked that he'd invited her.

She wondered if Winona Cobbs would be Stanley's plus-one. Maybe she could ask Winona about a reading at the quinceañera.

No, Shari couldn't wait. She needed answers to her big burning questions now.

She picked up her phone and did a search for Wisdom by Winona.

Winona answered her phone on the first ring.

"Hello, Ms. Cobbs, this is—"

"I know who you are, dear," Winona said.

That was a bit rattling.

"I'm hoping to make an appointment with you for a reading," Shari said.

"Of course you are. I'll see you tomorrow at twelve thirty sharp at my psychic parlor in my great-grandson's ghost tour business. Do you know where that is?"

The last time her parents had come to visit her and the town they'd lived in for decades, the three of them had gone on a ghost tour. Bronco, with its

Wild West past, was full of legends and interesting sites. People came from all over to go on one
of Evan Cruise's ghost tours.

"I do," Shari said. "And I'll see you there.
Twelve thirty sharp. Thank you."

Suddenly Shari wasn't so sure she wanted to
know what was coming. What if there was bad
news? Sad news?

What will I find out?

Chapter Six

Felix sat on an upside-down bucket beside a sweet brown-and-white calf in the barn at the Kingston Ranch and removed his stethoscope from his ears, letting it drop around his neck. It was six o'clock, and he'd been called in on his way home from the clinic for an emergency check on the poor little guy. The calf had pneumonia and would need to be separated immediately from the other calves and cattle in the main pen. The Double M had a "sick bay barn," so the calf would recuperate there.

"Is Snowball gonna be okay?" a little voice behind him asked. "Daddy? Will he be okay?"

The desperation in little Donovan Marconi's

voice made Felix's chest hurt. Ranch kids weren't supposed to get attached to the calves and lambs, but they often couldn't help themselves, naming them when working ranches didn't name their animals or treat them like pets because of the nature of the business.

"Well, let's see what Doc Sanchez says," Hank Marconi said to his son. Donovan was only four years old. Felix had gotten to know the sweet boy these past couple of years, a happy child who loved ranch life and animals.

He turned around to face the boy, remaining seated so he'd be at eye level. "I know this is really hard to hear, but this calf is very sick. I'm going to give him medicine to help him feel better. But tonight, he's going to need company and round-the-clock care. I'll know in the morning if he's going to be okay or not."

Donovan's tearstained face half crumpled and he looked up at his dad. "Can we stay with Snowball tonight, Daddy?"

"Sure we can. You and Mommy and I will camp out."

Donovan's face instantly brightened. "Hear that, Snowball? We're going to have a slumber party with you tonight."

Felix smiled as the boy wrapped his arms around his father's legs, looking up at him with such love and hope. How he managed to smile when his heart felt so shredded was beyond Felix. If he hadn't lost Victoria, they'd have a two-year-old now. Maybe a son like Donovan.

He and Victoria used to talk about children all the time. Even back in high school. They'd both wanted four kids, any combination, though Victoria liked the idea of each child having a brother and a sister. Each kid would be named using the initial of one of their parents. Dylan and Arabella for Felix's parents and Mira and Trevor for Victoria's. As they graduated from high school and then college and further school for their specialties, Felix in veterinary medicine and Victoria in dental school, they'd decided they'd marry young to support each other in their dreams and then would start a family when they were thirty.

It was exactly on Victoria's thirtieth birthday that she went to see her doctor for a physical, just wanting to hear that she was the picture of health before embarking on this huge journey. Two days later, her doctor had asked them both to come in to talk about her lab results. They'd both known immediately that something had to be very wrong. And it was.

One more test and the diagnosis had been confirmed. Ovarian cancer. They'd had just another year together. A year of fighting the cancer. Hoping. Praying. Fighting some more. And then three months of knowing she was dying, that there was nothing that could be done. There were second opinions and third opinions. Everyone was in agreement. But to the end, despite what he knew about cancer, he never lost hope that a miracle would cure her. Or just give them more time. And then time had run out. There would be no children named after their parents. There would be no family and no one. Just Felix.

Love, as even four-year-old Donovan Marconi was learning, was about loss, too. Felix was done with it all. He'd been so numb at his great-aunt's funeral in Mexico, Stanley sobbing beside him, clutching his hand on one side, his sister Camilla's on the other. His siblings, too, had been so shaken by the depth of their dear great-uncle's pain.

Yet despite that harrowing grief, Stanley Sanchez had found it in himself to fall for someone again. Felix couldn't understand how it was possible.

For Felix, the key to never hurt like that again was to not love again. It was that simple.

Yeah, he'd invited Shari to be his plus-one at the family birthday party this weekend. That didn't mean they were a couple—they weren't.

He was on his own, as he had been for the past

three years. As he'd be for the next three years. And beyond.

Felix wanted nothing more to do with love. Love just led to loss. Sure, he had family he loved. But he didn't have to *add* anyone to the list of those it would destroy him to lose.

The next day, Shari parked in the small lot at Bronco Ghost Tours and walked into the main building. Evan Cruise stood in the lobby, surrounded by around eight people, welcoming them to the tour. She gave him a little wave and headed down the hall, looking for a door with Winona's name. The moment she saw the purple door with the crescent moons and stars she knew she'd arrived. She tried the doorknob, but it was locked. Her heart sank at the thought that Winona wasn't available to do a reading, after all. Shari needed to know something. Anything.

Anything that would direct her one way or the other.

To giving up on love and going full speed ahead on her plans to be a mother.

Or to giving Felix a little more time to get to know her, to fall hard for her.

She'd thought she was settled on the idea of pursuing single motherhood. But another fitful night, unable to stop thinking about Felix Sanchez, about what *could* be, had her all confused again.

It was possible that the more they got to know each other, the closer they'd become. It was possible that he could fall for her. Entirely possible. And Shari always ran with *possible.* If something could happen, she'd help it along until it did. Glass half-full and all that.

He'd been in touch only once since his text about the family party he'd invited her to this Friday night. To ask about the kitten and if she felt comfortable fostering Page until at least the end of the week. He'd called the animal shelter and since their foster families were all spoken for at the moment, keeping the kitten with her would provide a good continuity while she got stronger.

She'd texted back her agreement and got back a smiley face emoji and one of a cat.

What she wanted was a row of heart emojis.

Gathering herself, Shari knocked on the door, and within seconds, Winona opened it. She had a completely neutral expression. Flanking her were two heavy purple drapes tied on each side. Winona wore a purple sweater with silver beads all over it, purple jeans, purple cowboy boots and a purple headband with a pin on it in the shape of a crescent moon.

"Welcome," Winona said. "Right this way."

Shari followed the elderly woman through the drapes and into a dimly lit small room. Antique floor lamps cast a glow. A small round table was in the center of the room, with a purple high-backed chair with velvet padding, and a pink one.

"Please sit," Winona said, gesturing at the pink chair.

Shari sat—and swallowed.

Winona was studying her. Her sharp dark eyes traveled all over Shari's face, even lingering at her right ear where her earring—a tiny green ceramic turtle—dangled. Now Winona was looking directly into her eyes. "You're here because you're unsure what path to take."

Shari gasped. "Yes. That's exactly it. That's exactly why I'm here." She leaned forward.

"For you, I simply have a question."

"A question?" Shari repeated. "But I already have a lot of questions. And no answers."

Winona raised a finger. "Ah. Yes. Maybe because you're not focusing on the *right* question."

Shari swallowed again. What was the right question?

"What do you want most of all, Shari?" Winona asked, leaning back in her chair.

"I—" Shari began, then clamped her lips shut. "I…"

"I'm waiting, dear. I *am* ninety-five."

Shari sat up straight. "Um, yes, of course. I don't mean to take up your time. It's just that I want a *few* things."

"Which is why I asked you what you want *most of all*. What is the answer?" Winona was staring at her hard now.

"I want Felix Sanchez to feel about me the way I feel about him," she blurted out—and promptly burst into tears.

"There you go," Winona said with a firm nod. She reached under the table and handed Shari a box of tissues. "The truth often brings tears. And clarity. Now that you know what you want most of all, you can go for it."

Shari took a tissue and dabbed under her eyes. "But it's not up to me. If he's not ready or willing to have a relationship, what can I do?"

"You can do a lot, Shari Lormand."

Shari was about to ask, *Like what*, but Winona was already standing up and walking toward the door.

"But I'll tell you the only thing you need to do," Winona said.

Shari's eyes widened. She wanted to either pull out her phone to record this or her little notepad and pen to jot down every word the woman said.

"Let that man see who you are."

Shari tilted her head. Disappointment socked

her in the stomach. That was the equivalent of *Be yourself.* Sigh. "Right," she said with a nod, trying not to sound dejected. "Be myself."

Winona shook her head. "Dear girl, thinking you know what's what is why you've been stuck. I'm not telling you to be yourself, though of course you shouldn't fake anything. I'm telling you to let Felix see who you are."

Shari took in a breath. "But I don't know what you mean by that."

Winona reached out and patted Shari's hand, her white hair glinting in the low lighting. "Well, don't think on it. Just *do.*"

"Do?" Shari repeated.

"Do," Winona said. "Listen, dear. That man is as lovely as his great-uncle, so I get it." Then she turned and walked away.

Shari smiled at the sweet comment, but found that instead of giving her a clear path, Winona's reading left her as confused as ever.

*** Chapter Seven ***

"Let him see who you are," Evy repeated slowly a half hour later on her break at Doug's, enunciating every word as though that would help her and Shari figure out what Winona had meant. The two were sitting at a table far from the jukebox and the dartboard and the noise of the lunchtime crowd. She'd needed her friend's advice—and a plate of nachos piled high.

Shari scooped up a tortilla chip laden with black beans, cheese, guacamole and sour cream. "I've been thinking about what she meant by that ever since I left her parlor. And I'm drawing a blank. I've been pretty open with Felix. I told him a little about getting my heart broken and dreams crushed. And I've told him what I'm looking for, so isn't that showing him who I am?"

"I think so," Evy said, popping a nacho into her mouth.

"And what did she mean by 'don't think, do'? Do what?"

"That Winona is very mysterious," Evy said. "But she's never wrong."

Did Winona actually *say* anything, though? Shari wondered.

Evy glanced up at the door and waved hello to someone. Shari turned to see Audrey Hawkins and her fiancé, Jack Burris, entering and heading for the bar. Shari waved, too. Audrey and Jack were famous—Audrey was one of the four Hawkins Sisters, rodeo competitors, and Jack was the younger brother of celebrity rodeo champ Geoff Burris and a star in his own right.

Evy sipped her soda, then sat up straight and snapped her fingers. "I've got it, Shari! Like with the kitten. You found a poor little kitty by herself in the library garden, rushed her over to Felix's clinic and then took her in to foster. That's showing him who you are for sure."

Shari was ninety-nine percent sure she was going to adopt Page, too. Hmm. Evy might be onto something there. Or not. "Remind me to ask you about kitten care later," Shari said, thinking of adorable Tina, the kitty Evy had adopted from Happy Hearts, Daphne Cruise's animal sanctuary. "But isn't my saving Page just being a decent human being? Being myself? She said she didn't mean that."

"But what else could she mean? That's showing him who you are. Isn't it?"

"I was kind of hoping for a more straightforward reading," Shari said.

"I think maybe Winona is just telling you that as you and Felix spend time together, to not be afraid to be vulnerable. To talk to him from the heart. Share what's going on in your life. I mean, your appointment at the fertility clinic was a big deal, Shari."

"It was just a first step to talk about how it all works."

"Yeah, and a big deal. Maybe Winona means that since you and Felix are friends now, you should take that to heart—as a friend, open up to him."

"But he's not even ready to date, Evy. The last thing he wants to hear about is my ticking biological clock at age thirty-four and what I plan to do about it."

"Winona didn't say anything about keeping your feelings to yourself. On any subject."

Shari ate another nacho, extra guacamole this time. "I think you're right, Evy. Maybe she was telling me not to hold back who I am."

Evy nodded. "Definitely."

Raised voices could be heard over at the bar on the far left. Evy turned around and Shari strained her neck to see what was going on.

"I'm not afraid of some dumb barstool," a big guy in his twenties was saying. "Let me at it."

"If you go near that Death Seat, we're through!" the woman standing next to him snapped.

Shari shook her head as the blond guy in a cowboy hat moved closer and closer to the haunted barstool. Didn't he realize it was cordoned off for a reason? She wouldn't sit on that thing for a million dollars. Because the moment she did and got her million, she'd somehow lose it. That was how the legend went.

The entire bar let out "oohs" and shrieks of laughter and various opinions were called out.

"So you believe in legends?" the guy said to his girlfriend. "Come on. If I sit on the Death Seat, I'm gonna get fired the next day or get food poisoning? Please."

Doug was drying beer steins behind the bar. "I could give you a list of the bad stuff that happened to anyone who sat on that stool. Take Bobby Stone.

A few years ago, he sat on that stool—just like you want to. And know what happened to him?"

The tough guy raised an eyebrow. "What?"

"He died. While on a hike. Dead. Just like that. But go ahead, sit on the barstool. Break your mother's heart. Lose your gal. Sure. No skin off my back."

The bar was dead silent.

"He died?" the blond guy repeated.

"Sure did," Doug said.

The guy backed away. "Well, I feel like standing anyway."

"You bet you do," his girlfriend said with a relieved smile, socking him in the arm.

He pulled her in for a kiss, which got cheers and wolf whistles from the crowd.

Evy rolled her eyes. "I love this place, but I'm really looking forward to my boutique's grand opening and working there full-time." She glanced around. "I will miss good old Doug's, though. Cowboys and all." Evy was very close with Doug and his family and would always help him out any time he needed an emergency waitress like today, but otherwise, she'd be hanging up her apron and order pad in a couple weeks.

"I can't wait for Cimarron Rose to open," Shari said. "Talk about going for what you want and getting it. I'm so proud of you. You're such a great role model. For me *and* Lola."

"Aww, thanks." Evy popped up and gave Shari a bear hug. "My break's over too soon. Go get your man, Shari."

Shari grinned. "I'll try."

She would try. Felix wasn't her string-Shari-along ex, who'd known exactly what he was doing. Felix Sanchez was protecting his heart—his big, lovable heart. It was up to Shari to show him he didn't need to.

By showing him who she was.

Shari let out a shriek, but because she was at Doug's, no one even looked her way.

That's it! she thought. *That's what Winona meant. Now I understand!*

She happily finished her nachos and her soda, then got up to head home to Page for some cuddle-time and list-making. A Friday night date at Felix's big family party called for a new dress. Something colorful for a quinceañera. Maybe some super high heels.

Oh, yes, Shari was looking forward to this more than she should.

Usually when Shari got home, Page would come shyly explore over near the door, then rub against her leg, and Shari would scoop her up to cuddle her. A little ear-mite meds, a gentle brushing, dinner and then more petting. While Page would then play with her favorite toys, sending her little plastic ball with the bells and her catnip mouse flying, Shari would tell the kitten everything.

What she'd found these past couple of days was that sharing her every thought aloud let her really hear what she was saying. Who knew that bringing a tiny bundle of fur into her home would bring so much joy and reward?

But when she unlocked her apartment door, there was no pitter-patter of little claws on the hardwood floor.

"Page? Where is my little cutie?" she called out. No Page.

No tiny mewing, no slight noise indicating Page was batting around a toy or scratching at her post. Her worry let her know she was now one hundred percent on adopting Page. As if there were any question.

"Page?" she called again, looking in all the rooms, not that there were many. Kitchen, no. Living room, no, including under the couch. Bedrooms, no. She wasn't under the bed or behind the drapes. She wasn't in the bathroom.

A chill ran up Shari's spine. Where was the kitten? She couldn't have gotten out this morning when Shari left, not without her noticing. She opened the door again, hoping it would lure Page out. It didn't.

She grabbed her phone and texted Felix.

I can't find Page anywhere. I don't know where she could be!

Be there in ten, he texted back immediately.

Relief flooded her. She spent the next ten minutes searching the apartment, the closets, under the beds and sofa again. Where *was* this little creature?

By the time Felix buzzed downstairs, Shari was in something of a panic. She pressed the button to let him in and paced by the door. When he knocked, she opened the door and ran right into his arms, tears in her eyes.

"I don't understand what could have happened," she said, her voice muffled against his jacket.

"Hey," he said gently, giving her a hug before stepping back. "She's in here somewhere. Kittens can get in crazy tight spaces. Don't imagine the worst. She might be fast asleep."

"But where? I looked behind the toilet. In the cabinets under sinks. In my closets." She bit her lip, her chest aching.

"Hmm," he said. "Let me think like a kitten." He walked in the living room and slowly turned around. "Kitty condo would be a draw, but she's not in the two little caves. Let's try your room." She trailed him into her bedroom, glad she'd tidied up this morning before leaving for work. His gaze beelined to the small shag rug on the side of her bed. Her fuzzy orange-and-white slippers were there, where they always were when they weren't on her feet. He walked over to the rug and kneeled down, then swiveled around the slippers.

Shari saw the whiskers poking out of a slipper. "Page!"

The kitten sleepily opened an eye, then both. Then closed her eyes and curled herself up into an even tighter ball and went right back to sleep.

Shari burst out laughing. "I'm so embarrassed. I didn't even think to check in my slippers!"

"Warm and fuzzy and smells like you," he said. "A kitten's happy spot."

"Smells like *feet*," Shari said, smiling and shaking her head. "I'm sorry I dragged you out here. Next time this happens I'll look in the slippers first."

"That's what friends are for," he said. "No trouble at all."

She heard the message loud and clear. Friends.

How can I show you who I am when you only see me as a friend? It's all the other stuff I want

*you to see. All the elements that make up a ro-
mantic relationship. Not just the core friendship.*

"Cup of hot cocoa as a thank-you?" she asked.

"I'd love some."

She was so aware of him following her into the kitchen. She wanted to turn and slink her arms around him, pull him close against her, kiss him...

Instead, she heated up milk and poured it into two mugs full of the fancy cocoa her mother had sent her from Denver.

They sat down at the table. Felix wrapped his hands around the mug and breathed in the scent. "Mmm. Reminds me of the best of my childhood. My parents always made cocoa when it rained or snowed or if I was feeling sad about something."

"Pure comfort," she said, taking a sip. "Were you close with your siblings growing up?"

"Definitely. Dylan's just two years younger at thirty-two, so we were close from the get-go, and I always felt protective of Dante, who's thirty. Camilla and Sofia are still in their twenties and fierce, so I always knew they could take care of themselves, even if we're still protective of them. They'll always be our younger sisters. Now with Camila married and Sofia engaged, Uncle Stanley is working on my brothers' love lives, too. They're both relieved he has a girlfriend now so he won't have much time to hand out their cell phone numbers and astrological signs in the supermarket to women who seem single."

She laughed. "Is that what he does?"

"Constantly. The night we…met at Doug's, he'd arranged for me to give veterinary advice to a single woman he met in the produce aisle. His eyes go straight to the left hand. No ring makes him move right in with the 'have I got a guy for you.'"

"Will he bring Winona to the quinceañera?" she asked.

"No doubt. My mother tried to set me up with a client's daughter, but that's where having a good friend as a plus-one comes in handy."

Clunk. Her heart dropped straight into her lap. So *that's* why he invited her—to get out of a blind date. Sigh.

"I'm glad you think of me as a good friend," she said, which was true. Having a friend was nice, but a good friend—someone you could really talk to, someone you could count on, was golden. She knew she was lucky to have hit it off with Felix Sanchez—finder of lost kittens. But she wanted much more.

"My mother won't rest till I'm remarried," he added, drinking more of his cocoa. "And because I'm the oldest, she's focused on me and not my brothers. She may slyly interrogate you at the party. This will be the first time I've brought someone to a family function since—"

She gave him a few seconds to finish or not and when he drained his mug, she reached over and squeezed his hand. "I'm looking forward to meeting your whole family."

He looked at her and smiled, and she could tell he was grateful she'd let that go. He stood up. "Well, I'd better be getting back. Early-morning ranch call at seven."

"That *is* early," she said. "Thanks again for finding Page."

"And thank you for the hot chocolate."

All too soon he was at the door, smiling that dazzling smile that made her knees weak and her stomach fill with butterflies. But underneath she could see he was still mired in the sentence he hadn't finished. He was bringing a woman to a family function. Friend or not, it was a first since his loss. And he was clearly heavyhearted about it.

The moment she closed the door behind him, she missed him. The object of her secret teenaged crush would always have a little piece of her heart—no matter what.

But then she felt a furry warmth at her ankle and looked down and there was the sleepyhead, rubbing against her leg. She picked up Page and cuddled her.

"What's gonna happen, huh?" she asked the kitten.

Page didn't answer, but she was as comforting to hold as the hot chocolate had been to drink.

Chapter Eight

The next afternoon, an overcast Monday, Felix was writing up his report for his last patient at the Bronco Heights Animal Clinic, a beagle named Josie who needed to lose a good ten pounds. He had two more dogs to see, then two cats, and then he was going suit shopping with his brothers since Dante had sat on something on a park bench that had never come out of his one pair of dress pants and Dylan had said all his ties were boring. Felix had a few suits and ties to choose from for the quinceañera, but he hadn't seen much of his brothers lately and wanted to catch up.

He also liked filling his time. Keeping a little

too busy. So he'd have less time to think about Shari and invite her places, like friends do. Coffee. Or a bite after work. The entire time he'd been in her apartment last night, he'd wanted to kiss her.

So what did this mean? He knew he wasn't ready for a relationship. Nowhere near it. He supposed being attracted to someone—very attracted, to the point that he dreamed about her last night—had nothing to do with whether he was ready to date. Attraction had a life of its own.

Then again, this powerful hold that Shari had on his thoughts and libido was new. He'd found women attractive in the past three years, but that hadn't messed with him.

And it wasn't just the pretty face and strawberry blond mass of curls and her interesting outfits and sexy body that had him all turned around. He really liked her. He could have sat at her kitchen table for hours, enjoying the view of her face, listening to her talk, appreciating that she'd taken in the stray kitten, but then that stark reminder about the quinceañera had sent chills up his spine.

In three years, there had been a lot of family functions. Big ones. Camilla's wedding, for one. Sofia's engagement party. Birthdays. Work promotions. Personal goal celebrations. Thanksgivings. Christmases. His father's thirty years at the post office. His mother had even thrown a party to mark being debt free on the salon. He'd never brought a date—even a friend for a plus-one.

So why now? Just to get his mother off his back about inviting her client's daughter? Maybe. Denise Sanchez had been getting as pushy as Stanley these past few months, his great-uncle egging her on.

Truth be told, he wanted to bring Shari to the party. Wanted to have his own person there as a haven of sorts. The Sanchezes and their various branches could get overwhelming fast with their big hugs and "*Tell me everything*," and though it had been three years since he'd been widowed, some of his aunts or friends of the family still went overboard. *"Oh, you poor baby, losing your high school sweetheart to that terrible disease,"* they'd say, hand to the heart, tears in the eyes. He'd needed to escape and take deep cleansing breaths outside, wondering if he could slip away unnoticed.

Now, though, he'd have Shari beside him. He'd introduce her as his friend, Shari Lormand, the children's librarian at Bronco Library. And then the busybodies would go pester his mother and sisters about what the "friend" label really meant and leave him be.

He was half-comfortable with the thought of taking her. Half not. He'd see how it felt to walk into an event with another woman. All dressed up. Clinking wineglasses. Dancing. He'd see.

"Wes Abernathy and Archie awaiting you in Exam Room Five," one of the vet techs said, handing him Archie's file.

Enough thinking. Time to get back to work. He was looking forward to seeing the cute pup again.

Felix tapped on the door and went inside and there were Wes and Archie, Wes sitting on the padded bench, and Archie, white and furry with brown spots, on the floor gnawing on a toy, an orange chewy dolphin with a squeaker in the fin.

"Good to see you, Wes," Felix said. "And this gorgeous dude looks great. No struggle as he went from prone to sitting. No wincing."

"He's a trooper," Wes agreed, his blue eyes tender on the puppy.

Felix scooped him up and placed him on the exam table. Archie was a calm pup, easy to handle.

Weston stood on the other side of the table, giving Archie a pat. "Sometimes I'm still amazed when I realize I not only have a dog, but a fiancée and that I'm gonna be someone's dad. Whodathunk?"

Felix glanced at Weston Abernathy, then resumed his examination of Archie, checking his legs and back. Wes was part of one of the richest families in Bronco. He was a good guy, but he'd been long used to getting whatever he wanted without lifting a finger—his looks, name and money just made things happen. But when he'd met Evy Roberts, a young single mom and a waitress at Doug's determined to fulfill her dream to open her own boutique, Wes had probably heard the word *no* for the first time in his life. Evy worked for what she wanted, and if Wes wanted her, he'd have to show her he was serious. About commitment. About being a father to her four-year-old daughter, Lola. And he had.

When Lola had fallen madly in love with the adorable furry puppy and Evy had been unable to imagine one more thing on her plate, Wes had adopted the pup so that Lola could have access to Archie anytime she wanted. Felix had known then that Wes had it bad for Evy and that his life was about to change.

"Big changes," Felix said, looking inside Archie's ear with his otoscope. "But I guess when you're ready, you're ready."

Wes looked at him like he'd grown an extra nose. "Did you say something about being *ready*?" He chuckled. "More like everything I didn't know I wanted and needed was suddenly right in front of me."

"So how did you know?" Felix asked. "I mean,

what made you realize that was what you actually wanted?"

Maybe he'd learn something about himself here. Answer some of these questions plaguing him the past couple of days.

"Well, I think you know when you meet some-one who's…everything. You can't stop thinking about her. She's got you tied in knots. She makes you think. Makes you laugh. Makes you wonder about things you normally don't think about. She makes you more *you*. And so you just *know*, even if you try to ignore it at first like I did. Like that ever works."

Felix smiled. "I might be doing a little of that myself," he admitted. "I'm not ready to get back out there. I'm not sure I'll ever be. But there's something about this woman that's got me all… everything you just said." He'd just said it aloud, admitted it. How was it possible to feel a weight lifted off one shoulder, but a heavier one dropped on the other?

He was grateful that Wes didn't ask who he was talking about. He was opening up but wasn't ready to divulge everything. "Damn, Felix. I'm really glad to hear that. Not that it's easy when you're in *No, I'm not and No, I don't* mode. But they just become part of you when you aren't even looking. The way I started feeling about Evy and

Lola felt huge. And scary as hell. But then nothing felt more right."

Felix was in the very beginning stage, he figured. At the point when Shari Lormand was sneaking inside his heart and soul when he didn't even know it. Lodging in there good. He was beginning to realize he had feelings for her. But he wasn't at the scary stage yet because he and Shari were just friends. That kept her in a safe spot mentally because she was technically off-limits, even if he'd wanted to slowly remove her dress last night and kiss her shoulders, her collarbones, along her neck until he got to her mouth.

A sudden lick from Archie on his wrist brought his attention back to the dog on the table. He finished his examination and gave the pup a good scratch behind his ears. "Archie is one hundred percent recovered. Just keep him away from mama bears from now on."

"Can't wait to tell Lola," Wes said, picking up Archie and putting him down on the floor and attaching his leash. "She's crazy about this pup."

If the Heartbreaker of Bronco Heights had fallen for a single mom and her little girl and just like that had become a family man—with a dog— anything was possible. *Even for you, Felix*, he told himself. But it was hard to keep an open mind with a closed heart.

He knew he wouldn't change overnight. So he'd just do what he'd been thinking ever since he invited Shari to the quinceañera. He'd see how it felt. To walk into an event with a woman. *Be* with a woman. Dance with a woman. Have family and friends assume they were a couple.

It wasn't going to feel right, that much Felix knew. And then maybe he could go back to thinking of her solely as a friend and move on from this whole sneak attack.

And if he was so sure it wasn't going to feel right, then why did having Shari by his side feel so necessary?

"Nothing but dead ends!" a voice grumbled.

Shari glanced over at the woman using one of the communal computers on the first floor of the library as she crossed the reception area Monday afternoon carrying a stack of children's returns. She recognized Sadie Chamberlin; she owned a popular gift shop in Bronco Valley, right near Evy's soon-to-open shop. Cimmaron Rose.

Sadie flung her long, wavy blond hair behind her shoulders and let out a huff before leaning back in her chair.

"Can I help with anything?" Shari asked her, shifting the books in her arms.

"Sorry for being loud," Sadie said. "I'm just

so frustrated. I'm trying to find information and I guess I don't even know what I'm looking for."

"Well, I'm not a reference librarian, but I could try to help," Shari told her. She set the books down on the desk next to Sadie's.

"Did you know Bobby Stone?" Sadie asked.

Bobby Stone—the man whose name had come up at Doug's when that show-off had wanted to sit on the haunted barstool to prove nothing bad would happen to him.

Bobby Stone. A few years ago he sat on that stool. Know what happened to him? He died. Dead. Just like that.

"No, but I know *of* him," Shari said. "I did hear that he died a few years ago."

Sadie took a breath and nodded. "He fell off a cliff while hiking in the mountains just outside Bronco. He'd told some folks he was going on the hike, and his belongings were found on the cliff. It was a pretty treacherous drop into desolate, heavy forest. His body was never found, but everyone thinks he took a bad fall—that he'd been drinking. The rescue operations just couldn't see through the dense brush down there."

Shari shook her head. "So awful. Did you know Bobby? Were you a close friend?"

Sadie looked down for a moment. "He was my sister's ex-husband," she said, her brown eyes sad.

Dana and Bobby got divorced six months before he died.

"Oh, I'm very sorry."

Sadie was quiet for a moment. "I lost my sister, too. She died because of a drunk driver last year. Both she and Bobby are gone. But the past couple of months, weird stuff has been happening."

"Like what?" Shari asked, sitting down in the chair beside Sadie.

Sadie glanced around, then leaned close to Shari. "Did you hear about the incident at Doug's back in July? Someone threw a big rock through the window. There was a note wrapped around it: *A Stone You Won't Forget* was written on it. No one had any idea why someone would vandalize Doug's like that—everyone loves that place. And whoever threw it was gone when everyone ran outside to try to find the culprit. The police came, but nothing ever came of it. I didn't think anything about it either until last month."

"Last month?" Shari repeated.

"There were flyers posted all over the rodeo at the Bronco Convention Center: *Remember Bobby Stone.*"

"Oh, gosh, that's right," Shari said. "I did hear about that. No one knew what to think of it."

"Well, when I saw those flyers, I remembered

YOU pick your books – WE pay for everything.

You get up to FOUR New Books and TWO Mystery Gifts...absolutely FREE!

Dear Reader,

I am writing to announce the launch of a huge **FREE BOOKS GIVEAWAY**... and to let you know that YOU are entitled to choose up to FOUR fantastic books that WE pay for.

Try **Harlequin® Special Edition** books featuring comfort and strength in the support of loved ones and enjoying the journey no mader what life throws your way.

Try **Harlequin® Heartwarming™ Larger-Print** books featuring uplifting stories where the bonds of friendship, family and community unite.

Or TRY BOTH!

In return, we ask just one favor: Would you please participate in our brief Reader Survey? We'd love to hear from you.

This FREE BOOKS GIVEAWAY means that your introductory shipment is completely free, <u>even the shipping</u>! If you decide to continue, you can look forward to curated monthly shipments of brand-new books from your selected series, always at a discount off the cover price! <u>Plus you can cancel any time</u>. Who could pass up a deal like that?

Sincerely

Pam Powers

Pam Powers
For Harlequin Reader Service

Complete the survey below and return it today to receive up to 4 FREE BOOKS and FREE GIFTS guaranteed!

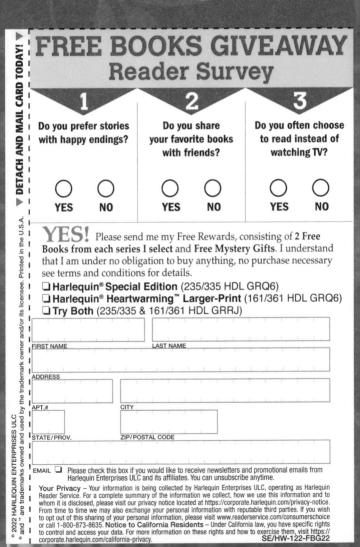

▼ DETACH AND MAIL CARD TODAY! ▼

FREE BOOKS GIVEAWAY
Reader Survey

1
Do you prefer stories with happy endings?

○ YES ○ NO

2
Do you share your favorite books with friends?

○ YES ○ NO

3
Do you often choose to read instead of watching TV?

○ YES ○ NO

YES! Please send me my Free Rewards, consisting of **2 Free Books** from each series I select and **Free Mystery Gifts**. I understand that I am under no obligation to buy anything, no purchase necessary see terms and conditions for details.

❏ Harlequin® Special Edition (235/335 HDL GRQ6)
❏ Harlequin® Heartwarming™ Larger-Print (161/361 HDL GRQ6)
❏ Try Both (235/335 & 161/361 HDL GRRJ)

FIRST NAME   LAST NAME

ADDRESS

APT.#   CITY

STATE/PROV.   ZIP/POSTAL CODE

EMAIL ❏ Please check this box if you would like to receive newsletters and promotional emails from Harlequin Enterprises ULC and its affiliates. You can unsubscribe anytime.

SE/HW-122-FBG22

▲ If offer card is missing write to: Harlequin Reader Service, P.O. Box 1341, Buffalo, NY 14240-8531 or visit www.ReaderService.com

BUSINESS REPLY MAIL

FIRST-CLASS MAIL   PERMIT NO. 717   BUFFALO, NY

POSTAGE WILL BE PAID BY ADDRESSEE

HARLEQUIN READER SERVICE
PO BOX 1341
BUFFALO NY 14240-8571

NO POSTAGE
NECESSARY
IF MAILED
IN THE
UNITED STATES

the note on the stone thrown through the window at Doug's. I think the two are related."

"I wonder why someone would be stirring up his memory now, though," Shari said. "Three years later."

Sadie nodded. "Exactly. Why? And who's behind it? I feel like there's more to come."

Shari felt a chill run up her spine.

Sadie stood up. "I'd better get back to my shop. Thanks for listening. I really appreciate it."

"Of course," Shari said. "It's unsettling. I completely understand."

Sadie nodded and then hurried out.

Shari had just moved back to Bronco when she'd heard about Bobby's death. The haunted barstool had taken on even greater legendary status because Bobby had sat on that stool just a few days prior to his death. A little shiver ran along her neck.

Shari was set to go on a half-hour break in five minutes. And boy, did she need it. She stared at her phone and tapped on Felix's contact info. She bit her lip. *Don't think, just do*, she reminded herself, Winona's words coming back to her.

Text him, she told herself. *Do it now. Before you lose your nerve. Friends text each other about meeting up for coffee. You're not asking the man on a date.*

Could use a cup of coffee. Double espresso. Just got chills over something.

You okay?

Yeah. Just…unsettled.

Meet you at Java and Juice in five minutes. I have a patient at the clinic in 45 minutes, but coffee and something decadent and an ear even for a bit might help.

You're the best, she typed and hit Send before she could delete it.

But he *was* the best.

Could he be better-looking? Shari thought as she walked into Bronco Java and Juice and saw Felix sitting at a round table. She wasn't the only one who thought so because he was surrounded by three women standing around him, holding iced drinks and tossing their hair and laughing at whatever he'd just said. As she slowly approached, she heard him say something about tiny Chihuahuas thinking they were the boss, and that they were, but a good training class or private trainer would go a long way in helping the relationship. The redhead in the center let out an exaggerated "Phew, I will definitely call this trainer you recommended."

Shari walked up to the chair across from Felix and smiled.

Felix stood. "Ah, my lovely date has arrived."

It was amazing how one line could give a gal hope and thoroughly deflate her at the same time. He'd referred to Shari as his *date*. But she knew he was using the term very loosely—as in coffee date—and to send the flirty trio on the way.

The women eyed Shari and gave her tight smiles, then thanked Felix again for his "so helpful info!" and left.

"Does any of them even *have* a Chihuahua is what I want to know," Shari said. Meanly. Jealously.

She usually wasn't a snarky person, but…she was a little jealous. When Felix Sanchez decided he was ready to date, he'd have a long line of attractive women to fill his dance card.

Felix laughed. "Actually, last month Stanley was talking me up at the supermarket to a woman he met in the frozen food aisle. She told him all about her sick cat and he assured her I'd meet her at my sister's restaurant that night to discuss the situation."

"Wow," Shari said.

"Wow is right. He had no way to contact her to cancel, so I felt like I had to go and somehow get through it and explain my uncle's habit of unsolicited matchmaking. Turns out, it was the woman's grandmother's cat that was sick—and twenty-one years old. Stanley hoodwinked me into a date. And trust me, I was not happy when I realized I'd been played—by both of them."

"Yikes. What happened?" Shari asked.

"I ate quickly, kept it professional, paid the check and then I told her I wished her and her grandmother's cat well and gave her my colleague's card at the clinic should she need emergency veterinary care."

Shari liked that. "Did you give your uncle a talking-to when you got home?"

"I sure did. He pulled out all the stops. 'I just want you to be happy. I just want you to find love. I just want to see you smile.' And let me tell you, Uncle Stanley can pour on the theatrics and waterworks like no one."

Shari smiled. "Hence why he got you to go to Doug's the night we met—the woman with the sneaker-chewing Pomeranian."

"Exactly. Let's go order before we run out of time. I spied something very chocolatey with my name on it."

Shari grinned. "Ooh, my name is on half of it if you want to split it."

"Deal," he said.

She practically floated up to the counter at his

side, all the anxiety that had gripped her after talking to Sadie dissipating.

They chatted with Cassidy Ware Taylor, the owner of Bronco Java and Juice, who'd recently married rancher Brandon Taylor, about the amazing renovations she'd recently made to the place. The spacious coffee and juice bar was now even bigger, with more seating and a big kiddie section with a train set and little tables and chairs for kids to color on. The Taylors had a four-month-old baby girl whom Brandon's stepmother, Jessica, watched during the working day. One of the wealthiest women in town, Jessica had surprised everyone by not only offering to babysit, but by being a doting caregiver and not minding if her pricey silk dresses were spit up on.

They ordered an iced mocha latte for Shari and a cappuccino for Felix, plus the Mississippi mud pie slice with two forks. Once they were back at the table, Felix cut the slice in two and they dug in.

"So what happened earlier?" he asked, taking a sip of his cappuccino. "Is everything okay?"

She told him about the run-in with Sadie Chamberlin. Shari sure hoped there would either be answers soon about the strange happenings or that they'd stop.

"Huh," he said. "That *is* strange. And I agree that the stone with the note and the flyers going up at the rodeo have to be connected. Someone doesn't like that Bobby Stone seems forgotten."

"She mentioned he was married to her sister, but that she died in a car accident last year," Shari said.

Felix's expression changed in an instant. His jaw went tight, his eyes troubled. "Yeah. Her name was Dana. She was young like Bobby. I remember thinking how damned unfair life is when I heard about her death. I mean, what the hell lasts?"

She flinched as she looked at him.

"I mean, my wife gone at thirty-one years old. Dana gone. Bobby gone. And then there are the breakups. The receptionist at the animal clinic was left at the altar, Shari. Stood up in front of two hundred of their friends and family. Because the bastard met someone else the week before and wanted to 'explore his feelings.'" He hung air quotes around the phrase. "And there's you."

"Me?" she repeated, hearing the choke in her voice.

"You got blindsided. It's why you moved back here, right? You were with a guy for five years and he strings you along and then you ask for what you want and need, and he says, 'Oh, this isn't what I want,' and he marries someone else a few months later? Love is—" He stopped talking, his jaw still tight, his eyes stony now. He shook his head and let out a breath, then picked up his cappuccino and took a long drink.

Whoa. In the space of a minute, everything had changed. From lighthearted quips about their Mississippi mud pie to…this. Had she ever seen him look this way, heard that hard edge in his voice?

She thought she was unsettled from talking to Sadie Chamberlin at the library? Now she just wanted to inhale the dessert and go home and cuddle Page.

"Sorry," he said, glancing at her. He let out a breath and dropped his head down for a moment, then leaned back in his chair.

"Love is everything," she said suddenly. Out of nowhere. "It's *everything*."

"It's the *end* of everything."

Oh, Felix. It's not. It's the beginning of everything.

Suddenly she wanted to order three more lattes and another treat and just sit with him for hours, letting him talk, letting him get it out. Maybe that was what he needed to do. And friends listened. Yes, love was everything and it was right of her to say so. Yes, she'd had her heart broken bad. But she hadn't lost a spouse. Of course Felix was down on love.

She needed to not forget what Winona Cobbs had told her. *Show Felix who you are.* She'd figured out what the nonagenarian psychic meant; now she had to remember that.

Felix wasn't her string-Shari-along ex, who'd known exactly what he'd been doing.

He stood up, taking his cappuccino. "I've actually got to get back for my next patient." He looked at her, his hazel eyes contrite now. "You asked me here because you needed a friend and now you probably need a drink. Maybe two. At least there's one last bite of the Mississippi mud pie." He gave her something of an awkward, sweet smile, and she just wanted to wrap her arms around him.

She stood up too and took his hand. "You can be yourself with me, Felix. And you just were."

He squeezed her hand, then let go. "I appreciate that more than you know," he said.

And then he walked out.

Chapter Nine

When he arrived home the night after their coffee date, Felix had called Shari to apologize for getting so intense, and the moment he heard her voice, he'd calmed down, felt soothed. Now, a few days later on a beautiful Friday night, he knew it was because she'd been right. He stood before the mirror on the back of his closet door and adjusted his tie. He *could* be himself with her. That was the hallmark of a true friend. That also had him feeling better. No matter how attracted he was, Shari was simply his friend.

He glanced at his reflection. Charcoal suit in pristine condition. Tie, not crooked. Black leather shoes shiny. He was ready. He grabbed the birthday card he'd gotten for his cousin Alejandra, in which he'd inserted a hefty check, and slid the envelope in his inside jacket pocket.

Downstairs was quiet, which normally would not be the case with a family of four getting ready for a big family event, but his parents had left a half hour ago to go "help" Dante and Dylan at their apartment, which meant making sure they were dressed to the nines. Now that Felix had a plus-one, Denise Sanchez had turned her attention to her younger sons and their love lives, and each unknowingly had a list of five women his mother thought would be just perfect for them, depending on the personal chemistry.

Felix was about to knock on his great-uncle's door, which was slightly ajar, to see if he was ready to head out, when he heard Stanley talking. He could see Stanley sitting on his bed, facing away from him toward the window. On Stanley's bureau was a photo of Celia taken just last year, with her trademark big smile.

"I know you're watching over me, *mi amor*," Stanley continued. "So I know you know that I am taking a date to the quinceañera."

Felix stood stock-still, holding even his breath.

"You would approve, Celia. Winona is a strong, smart, kind woman who doesn't take guff from anyone, just like you didn't. I'll tell you, she's been through a lot. *A lot.* I had tears in my eyes as she told me the story of being separated from her young love. They were still just teenagers. Not much younger than we were when we met."

Felix's chest constricted.

"Winona became pregnant and her family sent her away to some kind of home," Stanley continued. "They told her the baby died and she was so distraught that they institutionalized her. But her teenaged love, Josiah Abernathy, he found out that the baby *didn't* die and he vowed to find her—a daughter—before it was too late. Josiah was in his nineties and his memories were fading fast because of dementia, but he finally achieved his dream. Thanks to friends and family, Winona was reunited with her long-lost daughter, Daisy. They even share a home now. A whole family opened to Winona."

Felix loved that the story had had a happy ending. Last year, many were trying to figure out the mystery of who the long-lost "baby" Beatrix was, what had become of her. Felix had been amazed at how some important people in both Winona's and Josiah's lives had pulled together to find her—all for elderly Josiah Abernathy, who at that point was in a care home, and Winona, who'd lived in Rust Creek Falls, then. But Josiah had done it. He'd made it happen. Josiah had passed not long ago but the family had been reunited in spirit.

"Winona has a gift," Stanley said, still facing Celia's framed photo. "She knows things. When I'm with her, I feel like a combination of a teenager and the eighty-five-year-old I am. But I want you to know, *amor*, that no one will ever replace you in my heart. What I have discovered is that there is room in this old thing," he said, and Felix heard a thump, which meant he'd probably patted his chest. "The heart expands. But you always knew that."

The heart expands? Not Felix's.

Maybe that was the difference between him and his great-uncle. The reason why Stanley was able to date someone and Felix couldn't.

Felix's heart had shrunk. Not expanded.

He relaxed enough to actually move, though his muscles felt tight, especially in his shoulders. He went into the kitchen and slugged down a glass of ice water.

"I'm ready to dance the day away!" came Uncle Stanley's voice as he exited his room.

Felix left the kitchen to find his uncle looking especially dapper, his tie purple, likely to match his date's outfit, he figured. He glanced at Stanley's face; you would never know, unless you'd been eavesdropping, as Felix had had no business doing, that the man had just had a poignant talk with his late wife. His heart went out to his dear, sweet great-uncle Stanley. He loved the man so much. He had such an urge to pull Stanley into a bear hug, but his *tio* would know Felix had been listening.

"Ah, almost forgot," Stanley said, slipping past Felix into the kitchen. He opened the refrigerator and pulled out two square white boxes. "For the ladies," he said, handing one to Felix.

Felix opened the box. It was a corsage, blush-colored tiny roses. Stanley showed Felix's his—purple, of course, with silver bows.

"I wasn't sure what color to get for you to give to Shari, so the florist told me blush would go with everything."

"I wasn't planning on giving Shari a corsage. It's not part of the tradition anyway." He frowned at it, shutting the box.

"Oh, shush," Stanley said. "Since you're just friends, you can put it on her wrist."

Felix inwardly sighed.

"You look good, Felix."

"You, too, Tio."

Stanley clapped him on the back and pulled open the door. "Off to pick up my lovely date. See you there," he said, and practically skipped to his truck.

Felix got into his own car, the corsage resting

on the console, and drove to Bronco Heights to pick up Shari. He pulled up in front of her building. But it took him a good half minute to get out of the car. Another minute to press the buzzer. His collar felt tight.

He and Victoria had dressed up for a lot of occasions in their time. The junior and senior prom at Bronco High. Various family functions. New Year's celebrations. Their engagement party. Their wedding.

Now he was in his suit and tie and shiny shoes—and about to escort another woman to a family party.

Shake it off, man. You're taking your friend Shari to a teenager's birthday party. Calm the hell down.

Shari buzzed him in and he slowly walked up the flight of stairs to the second floor. She opened the door before he reached the landing and he stopped in his tracks. Whoa.

She wore a slinky red dress that skimmed her curves and swirled around her knees. Silver high heels. Her strawberry blond hair was loose past her shoulders. Every cell in his body went on red alert.

He swallowed his reaction and walked up the rest of the way. "You look nice."

She smiled. "You, too."

"This might be the first time I'm seeing you

without your glasses," he said. "When I think of you, I picture the strawberry blond curls, the round tortoiseshell glasses and interesting necklaces. Like the night I had the good fortune to be sitting next to you at Doug's."

"I wear my glasses to work every day, most places, really, so putting in my contacts makes me feel more party-mode."

"I get it. I feel that way about not wearing my white lab coat."

She seemed about to say something but a little sound made them both look down.

"Mew. Mew-mew."

Page was swishing around Shari's ankles. "Sorry you can't join us, kitty."

Shari picked her up and gave her a nuzzle, then put her down on her scratching box, where she immediately turned upside down and began clawing the sides. "I'm all set."

He swallowed again, watching as she grabbed her little purse with its long silver chain from the hallway counter.

Friends, friend, friends, he reminded himself. But he was still unable to stop looking at her glossy pink-red lips. The fullness of her breasts in the slinky dress and how the material moved with her.

But the biggest problem was that his intense attraction to Shari Lormand wasn't just about how sexy she looked in that dress.

Shari didn't know Felix Sanchez that well, but she knew this: the man could not take his eyes off her. Every time he looked at her, his gaze was smoldering. She wasn't one to flatter herself or see what wasn't there, either.

He wanted her. Bad.

Even if he'd told her she looked "nice." What he meant was smokin'. Which was exactly the word Evy had used when she'd texted her friend a selfie of herself in the dress she'd bought in a fancy boutique three years ago, the very first week she'd arrived back in Bronco. A promise to herself that someday, she'd feel okay again. Someday her heart wouldn't hurt. Someday, she'd wear it for the man who'd make her forget there had ever been anyone else but him in her heart.

That someday had finally come.

And did the man not say *Every time I think of you, I picture...* and then describe her trademark accessories?

He thought of her.

He pictured her.

He noticed.

She couldn't wait to get Felix Sanchez on the dance floor. For a slow dance.

But the moment they walked inside the festively decorated space, the band playing a popular song on the stage, they were surrounded by Sanchezes. Their debut on the dance floor would have to wait through quite a few introductions.

"You must be Shari," a woman with auburn shoulder-length hair, warm brown eyes and a big smile said, pulling her into a hug. "I'm so happy to meet you. I'm Denise Sanchez, Felix's mother."

Shari grinned. "Shari Lormand. It's so nice to meet you."

Before Felix could get a word in, Denise added, "Felix has only told me a little bit about you, but I'd love to know more." She glanced over by the buffet tables. "Ooh, there's no line at the buffet. Let's go load up before the teens stop dancing to this loud song and take all the mini empanadas." She took Shari's hand and led her over.

Shari loved how vivacious and friendly Felix's mom was. Her mother was polite but slow to warm up to people, which was fine, of course, but made for very awkward introductions.

"Mmm, everything looks and smells so good," Shari said. Her eyes widened at the end of the buffet table where a salad bar and range of Mexican and American dishes was set up, including an enchiladas station with mole sauce. "I can't resist enchiladas ever." She took one, then forked a bite. "Delicious. Yum." Two more bites quickly followed.

"No doubt," Denise said with a smile. "My daughter Camilla is catering the party." She craned her neck to try to spot her. "Ah, there she is, in the yellow dress," she added, nodding toward a beautiful woman chatting with a group. Shari had had contact at some point or another with all of Felix's relatives at the Bronco Library, just as she had with most of the town. But she'd never been formally introduced to any of the Sanchezes besides Stanley. Denise turned back to Shari. "Camilla owns The Library right here in Bronco Valley. And I understand that you work in the actual library in the Heights. I think I've passed you in there a time or two. It's been a long time since I've had a *niño* or *niña* young enough for the Children's Room."

Just like that, Shari and Felix's mother were deep in conversation between bites of the delicious food and the sangria Denise got them from the bar, chatting about everything and anything so easily. Every few minutes, someone would come to say hi to Denise, and she'd introduce Shari as Felix's date—with a smile. There was nothing sly in the smile, nothing but warmth. But from the smiles she'd get back it was clear that being his *date* was big and everyone at this party knew it.

Denise had been telling Shari a funny story

about the time she'd tried hair extensions on herself when the woman was grabbed away and Shari was quickly ensconced in another group. On the dance floor she could see Stanley and Winona dancing with old-school formality. Camilla and her husband, Jordan Taylor, and Sofia and her fiancé Boone Dalton, were chest to chest, looking up at each other with moony eyes. She glanced around for her handsome date, her heart speeding up when she found him chatting with two guys who looked a lot like him. Probably his brothers. She hadn't met them yet.

"Remember the tortoise," a voice suddenly said. "Like the eyeglasses you usually wear."

Shari turned to find Winona Cobbs standing behind her, picking up a mini taco and taking a bite. She looked spectacular in a purple dress with fringe at the hem, a silver scarf around her neck. Shari almost instinctively reached up to touch her glasses, then remembered she'd put in her contacts for the party.

"The tortoise?" Shari repeated.

"The tortoise." Winona took another bite of her taco. "There are a few hares all over this party. Sometimes that works, too. In it to win it and all. But you know what they say about slow and steady."

"Winona, are you trying to tell me something

positive about the super slow pace of my relation-ship with Felix?" Shari whispered.

"Yes, dear."

"Well," Shari said, telling herself not to blurt out what was on the tip of her tongue. "I don't know if I'm relieved or not because I've barely seen him since we arrived. Granted, that's been all of twenty minutes, but..." She wanted him at her side, intro-ducing her to all these people who were special in his life. Instead, he was...not.

Winona fixed her with her piercing eyes, then turned to gaze around. "He's avoiding the dance floor."

Shari almost gasped. Of course, he was. Why hadn't she thought of that? This was his first date since he lost his wife. His first dance floor with another woman. "Winona, I don't know if I should go hug him or just stand here and admit defeat and eat ten more mini tacos." She sighed. "I know I want to be a mother," she added. "I've been ex-ploring my options. But I'm so torn about giving Felix a chance or just going ahead with my plans."

Winona put down her empty plate, adjusted her scarf and nodded. "I understand. But slow and steady is always the best course. And if you were defeated you wouldn't be here."

Winona had walked away by the time Shari had processed the strange conversation.

"I'm sorry we got separated," came the voice Shari had been dying to hear in her ear.

She whirled around, her dress fluttering around her knees.

Felix had two glasses of champagne in his hands and gave her one. "Every time I excused myself to go find you, another relative grabbed me into a hug. I hope my mother and other family members didn't give you the third degree."

"Not at all," she said, holding up her flute.

They clinked glasses and they both took a long sip.

The band began playing a ballad that Shari loved. She almost asked Felix to dance but then remembered what Winona had said. *He's avoiding the dance floor.*

How could her heart not go out to him?

It's a good enough start to be here. He asked you to come. You're his date, as far as his family and friends are concerned. That's big enough.

"This is the most dumbest, stupidest, boringest party ever," a young voice said.

Shari exchanged a glance with Felix, both their eyebrows going up as they turned their heads slightly to the right.

Diagonally across from them, near the dessert buffet, were three boys, around eight or nine years old, in polo shirts and khakis. Looking very bored despite the cookies and treats heaped on their plates.

One of the boys crammed a cookie in his mouth, chewing around his words. "Yeah, and my mom said speeches are starting soon and if I burp on purpose I'm grounded for a week. I was planning to."

"You still should!" the third boy said. "I'll pay you five bucks."

"Ten," the burper insisted.

They giggled and high-fived.

"I would have been among them, no doubt," Felix said with a smile, then took a sip of champagne.

"Not me. I love speeches," Shari said. "Even the long ones that lose the train of thought. There's just something about someone standing up and saying how they feel—onstage, with a microphone. It always seems special to me."

More evil giggles erupted from the huddle of boys. "I know," one said. "Let's take turns bumping into the table with the ice sculpture. Whoever makes it fall over wins."

"Wins what?" the second one asked.

"Bragging rights."

"I'm in," the third said.

Felix grimaced. "This doesn't sound good. That

ice sculpture is actually an ice bust of the birth-day girl."

Shari eyed the boys. "I know what to do."

"You do? Are they about to get the librarian lecture in your sternest voice?"

"Nope." She walked over to the group, Felix coming up behind her. "Hey, guys. You might rec-ognize me from the Bronco Library. I'm the chil-dren's librarian. I could use your help, if you're not busy."

"Our help?" the one who came up with the bumping-the-ice-sculpture idea asked, his dark eyes curious.

"I'm putting on a Halloween Spooktacular Reading Party next month," Shari said, "and I want to tell only the scariest stories. *Really* scary. Could I get your opinions on the stories? They're short, just a few minutes each. And for listening and giving your thoughts, you'll each get a Spook-tacular gift kit at the library on Monday—but par-ticipating means you can't try to knock over the ice sculpture. Or do anything that would make the birthday girl or her mother sad."

The boys stared at her with wide eyes. "Okay," the ringleader said. The other boys nodded.

She turned to Felix. "Works every time," she whispered.

"You amaze me, Shari," Felix said, tucking an errant curl behind her ear.

Making her knees all shaky.

"Right this way, guys," she said, leading them to the back of the room.

She was sure Felix would disappear into the crowd again, but as the boys assembled their chairs in a semicircle around her, Felix took a chair too and smiled at her with so much in his expression that her knees felt wobbly again. Good thing she was sitting.

"Let me get your scare meters," Shari said to the boys. "Do you want medium scary or super scary?"

"Super scary!" they said in unison.

She nodded. "I thought so. Bronco is a town with a lot of legends. Scary legends."

The boys scooted their chairs in closer. So did Felix.

"Even the library has a legend attached to it," Shari said. "The basement mummy."

"Mummies are so cool!" a boy said.

"Well, the library basement mummy wasn't having a good day," Shari went on. "Someone did him wrong—a bully. And the basement mummy wanted revenge."

Three sets of wide eyes were glued to her.

"Wait, is the bully a mummy, too?" the ringleader asked.

"That's the thing," Shari said. "The mummy doesn't know. The bully could be a thousand-year-old bully. Or a kid from town around nine years old. No one is sure. Not all mummies are wrapped in gauze once they get out of their...resting places."

Shari had their complete attention, the demise of the ice sculpture forgotten as she continued the story. But when a statuesque blonde in a hot dress and killer heels kneeled down beside Felix and whispered something in his ear, Shari almost lost her train of thought.

When Felix stood and mouthed a *Sorry* to Shari—whatever that meant—she did lose her place. She watched the pair leave, the woman wrapping her arm around Felix's.

She frowned and leaned back in her chair.

"Wait," one of the boys said. "What happened to the library bully?"

"Yeah, does the mummy get him?" another boy asked.

Shari snapped back to attention and took a breath. She owed the boys better.

"Well," Shari continued, her heart feeling as if it was filled with water balloons, "the mummy was chasing him up and down the stairs from the second to the third floor…"

Three faces, waiting on her every word, stared at her. A flick of long blond hair caught her attention for a moment.

Felix was being led away and out the door.

Maybe the blonde was another cousin, she told herself.

Sure. That was about as possible as her *ever* having a romantic relationship with Felix Sanchez.

Chapter Ten

"How does this not go to your head?" Felix's sister Sofia asked him as she shook her head with a roll of her eyes. Sofia had watched him try to disentangle himself from the slinky blonde with a few pointed shakes of her head. His sister wore an emerald-green dress—one of her own designs—that complemented her long auburn hair, the late-afternoon sun glinting off her bare shoulders.

Felix and Sofia stood on the patio where the tall blonde had led him—on a ruse—to find a stray little dog she'd supposedly seen limping in the bushes separating the start of the property from the parking lot. *Oh, the poor thing must have run off,* the woman had said when they'd gotten on the patio and Felix had spent a good ten minutes looking for him, crouching down to peer under cars. No sign of a dog. *I'm Eleanor,* the blonde had practically purred.

Felix had shaken her hand and informed her he was going to go through the lot row by row to try to find the dog. It would involve a lot of crouching and might get her dress dirty. That was when the woman confessed it was all a flirty ruse to get him out here where they could chat. Would he ever forgive her? she asked, with a wink and a faux-sorry face despite the smoldering look in her eyes.

Felix had had it. He'd fallen for it—again. He'd been pulled away from Shari for the second time that night. And just when he'd finally pulled himself away from friends and family he hadn't seen for a while. A lot of those conversations had been about how sorry everyone was about Victoria, so maybe it was better that Shari hadn't been by his side for that. A few too many of those he'd spoken to had also lost loved ones.

"Wait, I know why it doesn't go to your head," Sofia said, leaning against the gray stone railing of the patio. "Because you've never been interested in dating the past three years, so you don't care that women are literally lying to get you alone."

"Well, I do care about that—it bothers the hell

out of me. Why would anyone think I'd find that a positive trait?"

"Boone's single brothers Shep and Dale get the same," she said, her rock of an engagement ring, as their sister Camilla had called it, shining on her left hand. Boone Dalton, Sofia's fiancé, came from a wealthy ranching family relatively new to Bronco Heights. Shep and Boone were the remaining single siblings out of five. "Though not ruses about stray limping animals. They get everything from sudden interest in the care of cattle to horseback riding lessons at the Dalton Grange. But I think they like it."

"Why are people so focused on other people's love lives?" he asked. "If I wanted to date, I'd be dating, you know?"

"Love is the one thing that brings the world together. People like it. They want it for themselves and for others." She eyed him. "And besides, aren't you dating now? I mean, this is the first time in three years you've brought a date to a major family function."

A waiter passed by with a tray of mini chicken taquitos. Felix took two plates while Sofia snagged them two glasses of white wine from another tray.

"To be honest, I don't know what I'm doing, Sof. My head says I'm not ready. But I can't stop thinking about Shari. We're just friends, and I mostly asked her as my plus-one to get Mom off my case about bringing the daughter of her best client. But it's more than that, too."

Sofia nodded. "No doubt. I've seen her in that dress. Shari got it at BH Couture, you know. The year she first moved back to Bronco. I was working in the boutique that day and I'll never forget her telling me she was buying it for the future, that she had absolutely nowhere to wear such an amazing dress and wouldn't be dating for, like, ten years after getting over her last relationship. But she wanted that sexy dress in her closet to always remind her that she knew the day would come when she'd put it on and know she was back."

Huh. He'd been so focused on himself that he didn't stop to think about Shari's own loss. She'd had dreams, too. And they'd been crushed, just like his.

Now she was here in that dress of…hope.

"Part of me wants to go with what I'm feeling," he said. "And part of me feels like it's wrong. That's where I keep getting tripped up."

"So take it slowly. We all can't be Uncle Stanley," she added with a smile.

Through the glass-paned double doors to the event room, he could just see Stanley and Winona dancing to a popular rap song that all the teenagers loved. In fact, they were surrounded by teens on the dance floor and only had eyes for each other.

He craned his neck around the crowd for a glimpse of that sexy red dress and strawberry blond curls. Ah, there Shari was, talking to Camilla and her husband, Jordan. Shari threw her head back and laughed, and even though he couldn't hear the sound, he knew it, could imagine it filling his ears. He watched as those three young would-be quinceañera-destroyers approached her. She kneeled down to be at their level and seemed to be listening intently. Whatever they were talking about, there were big smiles around. She high-fived each one of them.

A crack, a sliver, really, opened in his heart. Instead of the tiny space feeling drafty or outright cold, it felt…warm.

And as his gaze traveled down her curvy body in that dress, that sliver of space felt hot.

Shari. What have you done to me?

"Yup, you've got it bad for this woman," Sofia said, following his gaze with her own.

He couldn't deny that.

Sofia's eyes got misty, and he stared at her for a second as he realized why.

He squeezed his sister's hand. Sometimes he forgot how deeply his parents and siblings had shared his pain when Victoria had gotten sick, how devastated they'd been when she'd died. Uncle Stanley and Aunt Celia had flown in from Mexico and stayed for six weeks, Stanley barely leaving his side. For Felix to be interested in another woman was a big deal, and now the positivity, the possibility for happiness was getting him hugs and teary eyes from all his siblings, even Dylan and Dante, who hid that kind of thing well.

"I'm just so overjoyed for you, Felix," Sofia said. "Shari must be that special, you know? If she got in there," Sofia added, patting the spot where that sliver had cracked open.

"So maybe instead of standing out here, I should be in there."

She nodded. "Asking her to dance. But wait till this song ends."

He smiled. "I'll do that."

Dancing with Shari would either remind him of every scintillating moment during their one brief night together where they'd come very close to having sex—or it would remind him of everything he'd lost three years ago. He was rooting for the former.

But scared spitless of the latter.

The past half hour had been a whirlwind of telling scary stories and chatting with so many guests, including all of Felix's siblings. Then she'd been incredibly touched when the three boys asked her to tell scary stories at the library for their age group. She'd promised to add it to the roster and they'd happily run off to the dessert buffet.

Despite it all, she found herself glancing around the crowded space looking for Felix, but she didn't see him. Because she *did* know him, even just a little, she knew he wasn't in a coat closet having wild sex standing up with the hot blonde.

Because he was a good guy, a stand-up guy, and her date, just friends or not.

She looked around again, but didn't spot Felix. She did see Maddox John, a local rancher, all decked out in a suit instead of his usual jeans and Western shirts, standing by the buffet. Alone too. Shari knew Maddox from around town and, of course, because she'd seen him every now and then at Doug's. And she also knew from gossip that his wealthy parents were none-too-pleased that Maddox's older brother Jameson and his fiancée, Vanessa Cruise, were planning on a small homespun wedding instead of the huge event the Johns wanted. Shari couldn't help but notice a few women checking out the attractive blond rancher; given his reputation as a relentless flirt and serial dater, if he was here alone, it was because he wanted to be, for sure.

Maybe Felix wanted to be alone, too.

She brought her wrist corsage to her nose and gave it a sniff, the fragrance of the roses lifting her spirits.

"May I have this dance?"

Shari almost gasped as she turned around. There he was, gorgeous with his sexy dark hair and hazel eyes, in his charcoal suit.

Whatever had led to this dream of a moment, he certainly wasn't avoiding her or the dance floor right now.

The rap song had just ended and now the band was playing an old Celine Dion ballad that Shari had always loved, even if it cleared away the teen-agers. As Felix led her by the hand to the dance floor, she could see his uncle Stanley and Winona Cobbs dancing with her cheek against the lapel of his suit.

The moment she was in Felix's arms, all thought faded from her head. All she could think about was how good this felt, how good he felt, his arms around her, her head against his chest, her arms around his neck.

"I'm sorry I left the mummy story," he said. "I was as captivated as those boys were. It was a false alarm, too."

"Oh?" she asked. She pictured the blonde and mentally narrowed her eyes at her.

He nodded. "Never mind. I'm just glad I'm

back. I've…been thinking about doing just this for days."

She looked up at him. "Have you?" She almost squeaked the words. *Please be talking about slow dancing with me to a romantic Celine Dion song.*

"I might not be ready to date, but I can't stop thinking about you, Shari. Or wanting to kiss you again. So where does that leave me?"

Her legs did shake this time.

"I guess you might be a little bit ready," she said. "Just a tiny bit."

He lifted her chin with his hand. "Maybe so."

A surge of hope fluttered in her heart. She almost wished she had a hand free to pinch herself with, to make sure this wasn't a dream, that it was actually happening, but no way was she disengaging even a finger from around Felix Sanchez's neck.

"Did I mention how beautiful you look?" he whispered.

"You did tell me I look nice."

"Yeah. I meant incredibly hot."

She gasped, and he smiled, then leaned down and kissed her. And kissed her. And kissed her.

"I think they're more than just friends," she heard someone nearby say.

Felix had held Shari in his arms for the next hour, whether the song was fast or slow—and even through a line dance involving all the teens. They'd disengaged only for more of the delicious buffet and more chatting with his relatives. Luckily, outside of Felix's immediate family, Uncle Stanley's romance with his older woman was the real talk of the party more so than Felix's first date in three years. And then finally, the event had wound down and Felix was driving Shari home.

And *not* planning to peck her on the cheek at the front door and then leave.

Once inside her apartment, Shari slipped off her high heels, Felix's gaze going straight to her long legs. She picked up Page, who was rubbing her shin, and gave her a nuzzle and a kiss on the head, then set her down in her kitty bed.

"I love how much you love that kitten," he said.

"Who knew I was a cat person? I almost can't remember ever *not* having her."

"Yup, that's the way it works. They get you with those adorable little furry faces." He stepped closer to Shari and pulled at his tie. "I've been dying to loosen this tie all night."

"Let me help." She reached up and undid the tie, using both ends to gently tug him closer.

He looked right at her, the playfulness between them turning to smoldering, and then he kissed her. The only illumination came from a lamp and the glow of moonlight spilling in from the sheer curtains on the living-room windows. He pulled off the tie and tossed it on the sofa. Then leaned in for another kiss, very aware that Shari was undoing the buttons on his shirt, yanking the ends from his pants. When his shirt joined the tie, he pulled her against him, kissing her so passionately he heard her gasp and felt her almost droop against him.

He picked her up, her arms shooting around his neck, and she breathed, "Oh, Felix," in his ear as he walked toward her bedroom.

He set her down in front of the bed and whispered for her to turn around, which she did.

He slid down the zipper of her dress to the middle of her back, his hands going inside to move aside the slinky red fabric, and then the dress dropped, pooling at her bare feet.

"I thought white cotton was sexy the last time I saw you, but this…" He admired the delicate black lace bra and matching barely-there panties before he kissed the side of her neck, his hands up in her luscious hair. "And that's just from the back," he added on a whisper.

She slowly turned around. Her plunging bra left little to the imagination, which was fine with him. But before he could even reach a hand up to touch her creamy skin, her hands were on the button and hook of his pants, the zipper going down before the pants dropped at his feet. He stepped out of them.

"Nothing is sexier than those black boxer briefs," she whispered, her gaze down, down, down.

"Except you in these tiny black scraps of lace." He let his eyes feast on her breasts, her cleavage, her light perfume intoxicating him again. He reached up both hands to cup her face. "You're so beautiful, Shari." He could hardly believe it, but all he could think about was Shari Lormand. How she looked, how soft her skin was.

He was with a woman for the first time in three years. The only other woman he'd been with in his entire life.

"You, too," she whispered, closing her eyes.

They opened when he took off her bra and threw it to the chair by the bedside table. She licked her lips, and he inched her closer to the bed with his body. They gently fell onto the bed, him on top of her, and he slid down the length of her, stopping at her breasts to let his hands and mouth explore every bit. Then he moved farther along, kissing his way past her stomach and using his teeth to pull her little black panties down her legs.

"Felix," she said on a moan, arching her back.

He shrugged off his own underwear and then

was back on top of her, but she shimmied her way out and straddled him, giving him a hell of a view of her gorgeous body, her full breasts and the curve of her hips. He sucked in a breath, barely able to contain himself as it was, and then he felt her cool hand gripping him. Hard. He dropped his head back and groaned, and a delighted giggle erupted from her.

"Oh, yeah?" he whispered, his hands discovering every hidden inch of her, his mouth and tongue following as best as they could from the angle. The giggle had long since been replaced by moaning that was driving him wild. "Shari," he whispered.

She reached over to the bedside table and opened the drawer. He saw a box of condoms. Unopened.

"Every time I leave the house, I find out that my uncle put a condom in my wallet," he said on a chuckle. "More than three make things crowded so I move them to my drawer. I have no doubt there's a new one in my wallet right now."

"But is that one 'ribbed for her pleasure' and does it faintly smell of cherries?" she asked, opening the box and taking out a foil-wrapped condom.

"I really don't want to know the kind my *tio* has."

Shari laughed. "Allow me," she said.

"Oh, I will."

She inched down a bit to get to work, his head on her soft pillows, his eyes closed as he fought for control when her hands unrolled the condom along the very hard length of him. He actually could just slightly smell cherries.

And before he could open his eyes, she was poised over him, the sensation so powerful he had to grip the sheet at his sides.

She leaned down and whispered in his ear, "Are you ready?"

Dimly, he was aware that she was giving him a chance to get back in his head. But he was there already. And he wanted this.

"I'm ready," he whispered back and then set a hand on either side of her hips and guided her onto him.

He could barely hear her moan over his own groans. There was no way he'd last unless he was fully in control so he turned them over, Shari scooting up on the bed. He suckled on one of her luscious nipples, then the other, as his hand found the hot, wet core of her. And then with one last look at her beautiful face, he slowly let himself fill her, pressing down against her, his face buried in her neck, kissing her collarbone, then her mouth.

"Shari, Shari," he whispered as he thrust and

thrust, fighting to control himself as her long legs wrapped around his hips.

He could feel her hands in his hair, tightening, then her nails on his shoulders, digging in.

And then he lost all conscious thought as sensation after sensation rocked his body, her lips on his neck, her soft breath in his ear, followed by flicks of her tongue.

The nails dug in harder as he thrust harder, her back arched, her neck exposed, his name on her ragged breath.

And then his world exploded in the best way and all he could think was *Shari*.

Shari woke up in the dark to the sound of Page trying to claw her way up onto the bed, even though she had her own kitty ladder.

Which was how she'd become aware that Felix was actually standing by the window, wearing only his super-sexy black boxer briefs, his profile just visible as he stared out into the inky night— along with the hard set of his jaw.

Uh-oh, she thought. She glanced at her alarm clock: 1:24 a.m. This could go either of two ways. Either he was simply—not so simply, really— coming to terms with the fact that they'd made love and would come back to bed and spoon her with his face buried in her neck to give himself some privacy with his thoughts, or he'd say he had to go.

Don't leave, she thought. Prayed, actually. *Give this a chance, Felix. Give us a chance.*

If he did leave, she'd have to remember what Winona said. Slow and steady and all that. What had happened between them during the second half of the party and then continued just hours ago in her bed was fast. Inevitable, if you asked her. But fast.

Maybe now he needed to slow things down a little. Not sleep over. Not wake up with her. Take time to process that they'd had sex. And that it was a big deal.

Because it wasn't just sex. And they both knew it.

"It's okay if you need to go," she blurted out, pulling the quilt higher up on her chest. Then she mentally kicked herself. What if he wasn't thinking that? What if she was now putting ideas in his head?

He turned, his expression holding more emotions than she could sort out. She could see tenderness. But also tentativeness. He looked…off guard.

Maybe that was a good thing.

"You've got to see what Page is up to," he said, shaking his head on a chuckle.

She scooted over to the edge of the bed on her

stomach and looked down. And there was her kitten, all four claws stuck in the bed skirt and looking up at her with determined gold-green eyes. The poor thing hadn't gotten very far in her big climb. Shari disentangled her and scooted back to the headboard, sitting up against it, the kitten snuggled against her chest.

Oh, Page, what would I do without you right now? You're all that's standing between me and this man about to walk out the door and tell me he can't, he's sorry, but he can't.

She kept her eyes on Page, who was purring like a jackhammer. Shari couldn't bear even the thought of watching him walk around the room, picking up his clothes. Or sliding that pale gray shirt over his rock-hard torso.

But he didn't move from the window. She glanced over at him, and he was looking at her, and this time, all she saw in his expression was that tenderness. The tentativeness was gone.

Because he's about to say buh-bye. And feels really bad about it.

She held her breath.

"How about if I want to stay?" he asked, coming over to the bed and sitting down on the edge.

Her heart did all kinds of leaps in her chest. "That's good, too," she whispered because she could barely find her voice.

He slipped under the quilt, Page jumping out of her arms and onto his chest. "How does something that weighs all of three pounds pack such a punch of a landing?" He gave her a scratch on her head, and she crawled up one perfect pec to his shoulder and curled up at the top of his pillow between his head and the headboard and closed her eyes. "As long as *you're* comfortable," he said.

Shari laughed. Then she sobered up very fast. He was back beside her. He was staying. And suddenly *she* was the scared one. Her heart felt like it was pounding out of her chest and she turned away, onto her side, ridiculously happy and very nervous.

And then he turned too, molding his long, muscular body to hers, his arm around her. Felix Sanchez was spooning her.

If she had him, she could lose him. She hadn't thought of that before; she'd been too busy wanting him. Should she even be here? she wondered just as a tiny human combination of her and Felix came to mind, a baby boy with her strawberry blond curls. A baby girl with his dark hair. She knew she should be focusing on her dream to be a mother, but every time she looked at Felix Sanchez, thought about him, he was becoming more and more a part of that dream. Was she too hopeful about him opening his heart to her?

Slow and steady, she thought, closing her eyes as she felt Felix drop a kiss on her shoulder. Even if there was nothing slow or steady about how her feelings had snowballed. What began as a high school crush was now full-blown love. And Shari was here for it.

Chapter Eleven

Something was pushing on his head. Felix opened his eyes, aiming them at his phone on the bedside table: 6:22 a.m. He rolled his head back up on the pillow to see two furry paws kneading into his hair, the occasional claw making it feel like anything but a head massage.

He felt himself go very still. Because he suddenly remembered where he was. Shari's apartment. Shari's bed. He quietly sucked in a breath and glanced over to his right. She was facing him, eyes closed, a hank of strawberry blond hair over half her face.

He looked up at the ceiling. Were the four walls

of Shari's bedroom pushing in toward the bed? He sat up, the kitten scrambling from the pillow to his lap.

What had he said last night—exactly? Had he made any promises?

I might not be ready to date, but I can't stop thinking about you...

Okay. That was pure truth. He was okay here.

I guess you might be a little bit ready, Shari had said.

Maybe so, he'd said.

He didn't feel "a little bit ready" to be in bed with Shari right now under these circumstances. He certainly wasn't ready to cook breakfast together and read the morning paper, sharing sections while munching on bacon the way couples did.

He'd never been so glad that he had an eight-thirty ranch call. He would have to leave now. There would be no breakfast. He could process all that had happened. All that was happening now. That he was here in her bed the morning after.

All he'd do was overthink.

The kitten leaped onto Shari's ribs, and her eyes popped open.

"Oh, that felt good," she said. "Not." She looked at Felix. "Morning."

"Morning. I've got a house call at eight thirty," he said more abruptly than he meant to.

She picked up Page and sat up against the headboard. "You're like me—Saturday hours."

"You're working today, too?" he asked, relief flooding him. That meant they'd both be busy. No time for...anything. Like cuddling in bed. Or breakfast. Or making any kind of plans.

"Ten to five today," she said.

He got out of bed and reached for his pants, stepping into them. He was doing this wrong, he knew. He was *supposed* to stay in bed a little while. Kiss her. Chat. Not do anything to make her feel unsure.

Which was exactly what he was doing. And he couldn't stop himself. Because *he* was unsure and uncomfortable. When he woke up at 1:30 a.m. beside her and had gone to the window, he'd felt at peace—strange, not entirely himself, but at peace. Maybe it was the time of night or the dark room with the glow of moonlight. Maybe it was how comfortable he was with Shari. All he'd known last night was that the pull to get back in bed with her, to hold her, to let himself feel what he was feeling—which was a lot—was stronger than any urges to leave, that he didn't belong there, that he'd done something wrong by letting loose last night.

"I make a great Western omelet," she said. "But next time."

She looked so beautiful, her hair kind of wild, her tortoiseshell glasses on now. He wanted to tell her, but he just reached for his shirt and slid it on, quickly buttoning the buttons that she undid last night. A flash of memory got him, of her hands and lips on him, and he paused for a second.

Part of him wanted to stay a bit longer. He'd love that omelet and a lot of coffee. But a bigger part had no appetite and that feeling was back, that the walls were closing in, that he needed air. "Next time," he repeated, but he wasn't even sure if there would be a next time.

He crammed his tie into his pocket and sat in the chair by the window to put on his shoes and socks. "Well," he said, standing up.

"Know what Page thinks?" she asked, sliding her glasses up on her nose.

He looked at that gray, white and black ball of fur, her white whiskers glinting. "What does she think?"

"She thinks everything is just fine," Shari said. "This doesn't have to be called something or even mean something. We had a great time last night. A big first for you."

This woman is special. He walked to the edge of the bed and sat down, reaching out a hand to cup the side of her face. "You are absolutely lovely in every way, Shari."

He squeezed her hand and then he headed out, something in his head, in his chest, closing down, like a steel gate over the windows and door of a shop, as he left.

He didn't want to know what Page thought of *that*.

"Oh, no," Haley Butterman said, shaking her head, her precisely cut dark bob swishing against her chin. Shari and two of her coworkers, adult librarian Jemma Garcia and library assistant Haley, were at the coffee station in the break room. "That makes you the rebound sex, Shari. Rebound sex happens maybe three times, then you never hear from the guy again. Sorry."

Shari frowned and almost dropped her coffee mug.

"Um, first of all, Haley," Jemma said, glaring at the young woman, "you shouldn't make pronouncements about other people's relationships. And second, a little sensitivity, please. Especially when you overhear something and then barge into the conversation."

Haley shrugged and poured two packets of sugar into her coffee. "It's not my fault you were talking in the break room. And I'm honest. If you want sugarcoating, go somewhere else. If you want the truth, come to Haley."

No, thanks, Shari thought, taking a bracing sip of her coffee. Jemma was a good friend and they'd shared their triumphs and troubles from the get-go. But maybe she shouldn't have shared what was going on with Felix. It was his business, too. And he did seem like a private person. Then again, it was just as much her business. Her life. And of course she needed to talk to her friends.

But having Haley eavesdrop from the doorway before coming fully in—ugh.

"Just sayin'," Haley added before leaving with her mug and one of the scones from the box that Shari had brought in from Bronco Java and Juice.

"Ignore her," Jemma said, taking one of the mixed berry scones and standing up. "I've gotta get upstairs. I think everything is going to be just fine, Shari. I really do. You two took a major step forward last night. There's no taking back sex."

Shari smiled. "I guess there isn't. But there might not be more." That Felix had been uncomfortable this morning was obvious. She'd done her best to help, to let him off the hook, whatever the hook was to him, because dammit, that was who she was. A caring, compassionate person who knew when to put someone else first. This morning, Felix was that person. And she'd set aside everything twisting and turning in her heart, her gut.

At least she was following Winona's advice. Even to her own needs, her own detriment, her own impending broken heart.

"I think there'll be plenty more, hon," Jemma said with a warm touch on Shari's shoulder before leaving.

Shari wasn't so sure about that. In fact, she'd say there was a ten percent chance there would be more.

After Felix left this morning, she'd tried talking out her thoughts and feelings to Page, but the one-sided conversation didn't help. And then she'd shared it all with Jemma, who thought Shari should keep what Winona said at the quinceañera in mind—to a point. Slow and steady until it became too slow and made her feel unsteady. That was when she'd bow out. And return to her plan to make her dreams come true herself. The options for having a family and being a single mother.

Listen to Jemma and not Haley, Shari told herself. She and Felix had taken a major step last night. He *had* stayed over. There *was* no taking back sex. But there were endings. And that could be coming.

Shari bit her lip, then picked up her chocolate coconut scone and took a bite. Maybe Haley was right, though—and Shari couldn't really think of this as a major step for her and Felix. It was more a major step for Felix himself.

No, that was wrong. That took Shari out of the equation and made this about Felix. He hadn't been alone in that bed last night. She hadn't kissed herself at the quinceañera.

Sometimes love and romance was about the right place and the right time. If Shari had been sitting next to Felix Sanchez at Doug's a year ago, he probably wouldn't even have accepted her offer to drop him home, let alone invited her in for churros. Then again, maybe he would have. Maybe the chemistry between them, even if friendship was as far as he'd go, would have had the same effect. Maybe it wasn't about time and place so much as the people involved. Take her ex-boyfriend. He'd strung Shari along for five years because he recognized, at some level, maybe even not consciously, that she wasn't really *it* for him. Then he met someone who was and he knew it. Which was why he'd married her three months later.

Huh. She hadn't really thought about it like that before.

Still once again, Shari's future was a big question mark.

What she needed was another session with Winona.

She's not going to tell you what you need to hear, Shari. You know that.

But Winona was wise. Her business was called Wisdom by Winona, not 100% Psychic Glimpses into Your Future. *So call her.*

She got up and poked her head out of the break room to make sure that Haley wasn't around, then sat back down with her phone and pressed in Winona's number.

"Hello, Shari."

"I hope I'm not interrupting you, Winona, but—"

"Actually, I've got five minutes before Stanley is picking me up for apple picking. My favorite are Honeycrisps. Costly but delicious."

Shari hesitated. Was Winona trying to tell her something? That her relationship with Felix was going to be delicious—obviously, à la last night—but costly as in to her heart and well-being?

She shook her head at herself. Haley had gotten in her head and that was all. Winona was talking about apples and only apples!

"Did you have a question for me, dear?" Winona asked.

"Not so much a question but a… but…well—" She let out a breath. "I'm just a little unsure of myself."

"I can plainly hear that."

"Any advice? Wisdom?" Shari asked, realizing

she was waiting on Winona's every word, banking too much on hope.

That wasn't right. *This* wasn't right.

She was going to let her feelings for a man who was only half-available shake her up like this? When she might end up brokenhearted for another three years? Or forever?

She scoffed at her own words. Half-available. As if there were such a thing. A person was either available or not.

But there would never be another Felix Sanchez. There might be a perfectly fine guy in the wings. But Felix was…special.

"Listen, Shari. Life, every bit of it, is full of ups and downs. From the happiest of days to heartbreak so painful I thought I wouldn't survive it. In my ninety-five years, I've felt it all."

Shari had no doubt that was true. She sucked in a breath.

"All I can tell you is that you can't control other people," Winona said. "You can only control yourself. You know what's right for you. You know what to do. Do that."

Shari's shoulders slumped. "I'd really rather you just *tell* me what to do." And think. And feel.

"But you already know, dear," Winona said. Shari could hear a doorbell. "There's my Stanley. Bye, now."

Did she know what to do when it came to Felix?

Her phone pinged with a text a few minutes later, from Winona. I forgot to say something. Don't think on it too much. Just do.

Actually, that made Shari feel better because she'd been sitting there, wracking her brain for what she supposedly knew. *Just do.*

But do what?

Maybe no one noticed that I didn't come home last night, Felix thought as he unlocked the front door of the Sanchez family home later that afternoon. He'd had a long day—three ranch calls this morning—one to the Double J, the John family ranch, where Maddox John had assisted him in saving a very ill foal—and then he'd been the doctor on call for the past four hours at the clinic. He hadn't gotten much sleep last night and just wanted to fall into bed and hopefully take a good hour's nap.

Anything not to process his evening with Shari. He'd been thankfully distracted all day. Not that he hadn't thought of her or hadn't had very vivid flashes of memory. The only thing he knew for sure when it came to Shari Lormand was that he didn't want to hurt her. *Couldn't* hurt her.

So did he move forward with seeing her as more than friends? They'd crossed that line—*he'd* crossed that line. And he wanted to be with her again. But Shari wasn't looking for something casual and he wasn't looking to jump in to anything serious. He didn't know what he was doing.

But being with Shari had felt good and felt right last night. This morning, in the cold light of day, he'd been out of sorts, his skin had felt tight, and he'd just wanted to leave. But that seemed like part of the process. He wondered what she was doing right now. What she was thinking. Had he made her feel bad when he'd left? Uncertain? She'd been so kind last night, this morning again, by telling him it was okay to leave if he needed to, by telling him they didn't have to label what was going on between them. Why couldn't he be more like that and just let himself explore this? Why was it so damned hard for him?

As Felix opened the door to the house, he glanced at the driveway for Stanley's truck, and there it was. He sighed. His *tio* would be full of questions and sly smiles about his big date last night. Felix had kissed Shari right in the middle of the dance floor too, so if Stanley hadn't seen that with his own eyes, family gossip would have made sure he knew about it. At least his parents' cars were gone. He'd chat with his uncle for a minute, then disappear upstairs to take that nap, make a pre-dinner snack of delicious leftovers his parents had likely brought home from the quinceañera, and then he'd be more ready to face the barrage of questions he'd get hit with.

When he stepped inside, he could see his uncle Stanley sitting on the sofa in the living room, an old photo album open on his lap. And unless Felix was mistaken, Stanley Sanchez was wiping under his eyes. As though he was crying.

Felix frowned and peered closely at Stanley as he closed the door and headed into the living room. "Tio? Everything okay?"

Stanley quickly shut the album and put it behind him, as if hiding it. He quickly swiped under his eyes again with his knuckles.

"Looking at old family pictures?" Felix asked, not wanting to let this go. His great-uncle was a dramatic, emotional person, but if Stanley was crying and not wanting Felix to know he was looking at photos, something was wrong.

Stanley took a breath and pulled the album back out and onto his lap. "After the quinceañera, I went to Winona's like I have every night since we met." He bit his lip and clamped his lips shut.

"Did you have an argument or something?" Felix asked.

Stanley shook his head. He picked up his drink from the coffee table and took a sip. "We were standing on the back deck, enjoying the night, and all of a sudden I saw a shooting star." He covered his face with his hands and then wiped under his eyes.

Felix went over to the couch and sat down, putting his hand on his uncle's arm. Stanley took in a breath, his mouth down-turned, his shoulders slumped.

"The night I proposed to Celia, sixty years ago," Stanley continued, "I'd seen a shooting star. I saw it and I knew it was a sign from the heavens that I had to ask her to marry me that minute. I ran to her house even though it was close to midnight and woke up her parents. I asked for permission to marry the most wonderful woman in the world. I told them a shooting star had blessed our union. Her parents said yes. And so did my Celia. We got married the next day."

"I've always loved that story," Felix said gently, knowing there was more to come, the part that had made Stanley feel so awful.

"Seeing a shooting star is a once-in-a-lifetime thing," his uncle went on. "But there it was again, right in the sky last night, just when I was looking up. I saw that star and I told Winona I wasn't feeling well and that I had to leave."

Felix was bursting to ask why, but he held it back. He had to let his uncle talk at his own pace.

Stanley shook his head and swiped under his

eyes again. "I think that star was Celia. She must have been so hurt, Felix." His uncle hung his head and covered his eyes with his hands. "She must have felt so hurt and betrayed that I was with another woman—that I have a girlfriend."

Oh, Tio. Felix felt his own eyes tear up, his throat clogging. "Uncle Stanley," he said, leaning closer and pulling the man into his arms. His great-uncle sagged against him, sobbing.

"Do you want to know a secret?" Felix said, pulling away a bit so that his uncle could see his face.

Stanley sat back and leaned his head against the cushion. He nodded.

"The morning that Victoria died, she told me she wanted me to find love again, that I shouldn't be alone."

Stanley tilted his head. "Really?"

Felix nodded. "When she fell asleep a few minutes later, I went into the bathroom and broke down crying. I thought, *never.* I'll never love another woman. I was hurting bad—but I was angry, too. Not at Victoria. At the world. At everything. But until right now, I never stopped to think that my vow of *never* meant I wasn't honoring what she wanted for me for the future."

He honestly hadn't considered that until the words came out of his mouth. But now he saw how true they were. He might not be ready for a relationship, but he'd finally taken *never* off the table. Last night, in fact.

"What are you saying?" Stanley asked.

"That I think Aunt Celia would also want you to find love again. To be happy. To not be alone."

Stanley looked at him, his dark eyes so heavy with emotion. "You think the shooting star was your great-aunt Celia giving her permission like her parents did all those years ago?"

Felix was so choked up he couldn't find his voice for a minute. He nodded. "That's exactly what I think."

"We had a date to go apple picking today," he said. "But I canceled. I told her in person, at least. Not that I told her anything. I just stood there, and no words would come. Winona took my hands and kissed both of them and said it was okay. And then I came back home. Maybe I should go try to explain."

Felix had a feeling that Winona already knew exactly what was going on with her new beau. "I think that's a great idea."

Stanley brightened and stood. "I'll see you later, Felix. And then I want to hear all about your night." A bit of the twinkle was back in his eyes.

As his uncle left, Felix headed upstairs, but he had a feeling he wouldn't be able to nap for a second. His head was a jumble. And tomorrow night was the weekly Sanchez family dinner, tradition for decades. His love life would be a big topic.

He did want his uncle to have love in his life again. Someone special to share in all the big and small moments. Just like his family wanted for him. But he also knew why Stanley was struggling over that shooting star.

Felix went into his room and changed into a T-shirt and sweatpants and then slid under the comforter and closed his eyes for that nap. But thinking about Shari kept him wide-awake.

Chapter Twelve

At six o'clock, Shari had settled on her sofa with Netflix, a bowl of popcorn for dinner and a chenille throw over her, when her phone rang. She paused *The Great British Baking Show* and hoped it was Felix with a sweet sentiment. Something. Anything.

She hadn't heard from him today. No mocha latte. No churros. No note. Not even an *All best*. That was probably a good thing, though. The first time they'd spent the night together, even if they hadn't had sex, he'd felt compelled to send her something that showed he was a gentleman—the coffee and treat—but that he had regrets, hence the professional sign-off from hell. Today, though, he wasn't trying to say anything or put any distance between them; he'd likely spent the day processing how he was feeling.

You can't take back sex, she recalled Jemma saying.

But you could say goodbye. And every time her phone rang or pinged and it wasn't Felix, she actually felt *relieved*.

She slowly slid the phone closer on the coffee table.

Not Felix. Evy.

"Hi, Evy," Shari said.

"Hi, and I have a huge favor to ask. My dad is out for the evening, and our sitter just canceled on us at the last second and we're expected at a rancher's association fundraiser in a half hour. Lola's very hopeful that you might be available? She's dying to play with Page."

Shari glanced around at her empty house—well, empty except for Page. Evy had a full house with her dad and Lola and Tina the kitten and all their toys, and soon Evy and Lola would be moving to the Flying A ranch when she married Wes Abernathy.

Shari smiled and said, "Sure thing. We'll make cookies instead of watching people make cookies. Page is looking forward to the extra attention."

"You're the best," Evy said, sighing with relief.

Shari adored four-year-old Lola. Plus, babysitting meant experience around children in a home setting. The one time Shari had babysat and put the little girl to bed, reading her a story and giving her a kiss on the forehead, her heart had felt close to bursting with how much she wanted to be a mother herself. Tonight, she'd really focus on all that was involved in taking care of a child, even for just a few hours. Evy and Wes would no doubt pick up Lola way past her bedtime, but apparently she transferred easily from bed to car to bed.

Which had her imagining herself and Felix picking up *their* child from the sitter's—maybe "Auntie" Evy and "Uncle" Wes—Felix carefully carrying her to their car and then Shari laying her down in her cozy bed with her favorite stuffed animal, Page curled at her side. The two of them watching their child sleep, the rise and fall of the little chest, and they'd be overcome with emotion, wrapping their arms around each other before tiptoeing out.

Love. Family.

The fantasy had her so wistful that she had to suck in a breath and bring the chenille throw up to her neck to comfort her. Everything in her life was a big maybe right now.

Her phone pinged again. And this time it *was* Felix. She closed her eyes, not wanting to look.

Not that Felix would say much in a text. If he had regrets, they sure wouldn't come that way.

She opened her eyes and grabbed her phone.

Thought I'd bring by a pizza and we could talk.

She swallowed. Talk about…what? That he was very sorry, but he just wanted to be friends? That he had the time of his life last night and wanted more of that?

I'm babysitting for Evy and Wes tonight. Lola's coming to my place to play with Page.

Three little dots appeared. And stopped. Then started. Then stopped. Then started.

In that case, I'll get two pizzas. One plain and one pepperoni.

Interesting. She expected him to say: *Another time, then.*

I don't think we'll be able to talk with a four-year-old around, she texted back.

Maybe that's better, he wrote.

Huh. Maybe it was.

* * *

Crazy thing was, Felix didn't even know what he'd planned to talk about when he'd sent that text. He only knew he wanted to be with Shari, see her, be in talking range if subjects came up that should be discussed. He didn't want to *not* call her, not see her just because he was unsure of what the hell he was doing. Or feeling.

And Lola would be a buffer. Her being there was probably a plus. He could spend time with Shari yet the evening would be kept light out of necessity for little ears.

As he parked in front of Shari's building, he sent his uncle a quick text.

How are things? He added the emoji of the smiley face wearing a cowboy hat. His uncle used that in every text, no matter the content.

Bueno, Stanley texted back. Winona says honesty is everything. We just made popcorn and are planning a Hitchcock marathon, starting with *Rear Window.*

He smiled at the notion of Stanley and Winona cuddled on the couch watching old thrillers. But he was hoping for a little more elaboration. Felix knew honesty was always the best policy. And sharing how seeing that shooting star had made Stanley feel had very likely brought him and Winona even closer.

But how honest could he be with Shari when he wasn't all that sure what he was feeling? No one wanted to hear *I don't know, I can't say, can't we just*.

Especially not Shari, who'd dealt with that for five years and then got badly hurt.

He wouldn't mind having a reading with Winona. Maybe he should set that up. Get some clarity, a little guidance. And now that Winona and Stanley were a couple, maybe the psychic would have some extra insight for her paramour's grand-nephew. Hey, he'd take what he could get.

He got the delicious-smelling pizzas from the passenger seat and headed into Shari's building. When he got up to the landing, he could see Shari and Lola, holding the kitten, waiting for him in the doorway.

"Doc Felix, does Page like pizza?" Lola asked, her long dark hair in a ponytail and her green eyes bright.

Felix was amazed at how sweet and docile the kitten was, allowing Lola to hold her. The little girl had some great training in baby pet care when Wes had adopted the puppy she'd fallen in love with and Evy had adopted Tina the kitty. Evy and Wes had both taught her how to approach Archie and Tina, how to hold them, how to treat them. She'd clearly shown that same care with Page under Shari's supervision.

"Even though pizza is so good, it's not good for kittens," he said. "And that was a really smart question to ask me."

"Page likes me," Lola said, giving the kitten's head a nuzzle.

"She sure does," Felix agreed, smiling at the girl and up at Shari.

Even with the aroma of the pizza, he still got hints of Shari's sexy perfume, that slight sandalwood scent. She wore a V-neck hunter-green sweater and skinny jeans that hugged her curves and he had to drag his eyes off her body—the body he'd explored every inch of last night.

He focused on her socks—with little books all over them—no shocker there. Lola was wearing a similar outfit but her socks had little puppies on them.

"Well, let's head into the kitchen and attack that pizza," Shari said, clearly aware that his gaze had lingered on her body. There was nothing *All best, Felix* about the way he'd looked at her. He was getting to know her well, and there were questions in her eyes. What did he mean by *We should talk?* What did *Maybe it's better that we can't* mean? What was going to happen?

"Yay!" Lola said. "Sorry you can't have any,

Page," she told the kitten solemnly as she set her down. "Maybe when you're four years old like me."

As Felix opened the two boxes on the round table and they all helped themselves, Lola's excited chatter about the cheese being the cheesiest and the crust being the crustiest had him suddenly flashing back to those conversation with Victoria about starting a family. Hopes, dreams, plans. Gone in a second in a doctor's office.

When would he look at a child and not think about what he'd lost?

"Mmm, this is so good," Lola said, a stretchy piece of mozzarella extending from her mouth to the slice in her hand.

Shari laughed. "Agreed. Bronco Brick Oven Pizza is my favorite ever."

Lola finished her big bite. "Doc Felix, are you and Shari married?"

Felix froze for a second. He shook his head. "We're friends. Like you and Page."

"One of you is a kitten?" Lola asked, looking from Felix to Shari. "You don't have whiskers, Doc Felix. But Shari doesn't, either."

"Yeah, Felix, which one of us is the kitten in this friendship?" Shari asked playfully.

He quickly took a big bite of his slice of pepperoni and then pointed to it, making an exaggerated facial expression for why he couldn't respond to either of them.

How this conversation went from potentially awkward to funny did a lot of good for how heavyhearted he'd been feeling a couple of minutes ago.

After they finished eating, they went into the living room to play Lola's favorite board game, Candy Land. Sitting on the floor on the soft area rug, they explored the Peppermint Stick Forest and Peanut Brittle House and Gumdrop Mountain. Three times. Lola won the first game, Shari the second, Felix the third, and now Lola was trying for her second victory.

"Uh-oh, Doc Felix," Lola said, lying on her tummy. "You landed on a licorice, so you lose a turn! Are you sad?" She peered at him closely.

"Nope. Not sad at all. Know why?"

She tilted her head. "Because you don't like licorice?"

"Actually, I do. Red *and* black. But I'm not sad because I'm having such a good time playing this game with you and Shari."

"And Page," Lola added.

"And Page," Felix agreed.

He glanced over at Shari and the look on her face sent a chill up his spine. Everything about her expression was wistful, yearning. He knew she wanted a family, a husband and a child, but that she was worried time might be running out so she was exploring her options.

That expression told him he couldn't screw around here. Whatever was going on between him and Shari wasn't just about him—and he kept forgetting that.

He was grateful when Lola won the game and turned her attention to Page and trying to count how many toes were on each paw. Because he was kind of worried about the expression that had to be on his face, and Lola missed nothing.

Neither did Shari.

Lola let out a giant yawn. Then another. "I'm not tired," she said.

Shari smiled at her. "I have a great idea. Lola, why don't you help me put the pieces back in the game box, and then you'll pick out a book from my collection for my most special visitors."

"Yay!" Lola said, clapping her hands. She quickly helped pack up the game and then bolted up and slipped her hands into Shari's. "Can I pick the book now?"

Shari nodded, and they headed toward the bookshelf, where it looked like Shari kept a row of children's books.

Lola took out a few and slid them back and

then took out another, her face lighting up. "It's about a kitten! Doc Felix, will you read it to me?" Lola asked.

Felix felt a pinch in the region of his heart. *Let it all go*, he told himself. *This is not your and Victoria's almost child. This is not your and Shari's would-be future. This is just a sweet little girl, the daughter of mutual friends, asking you to read her a bedtime story.*

"I'd love to," he told her, and she handed him the book.

"Let's go wash up while Doc Felix gets the story reader chair all set up beside your bed," Shari said.

Felix took the book into the guest room. He hadn't been in here before. He moved the rocking chair from the window over to the bed, where Lola had already set her favorite stuffed animals. Her little backpack with flowers on it was on the dresser.

He sucked in a breath, unsure why he couldn't stop his head from going there. From the almost and the what-ifs and the losses.

He tried to shake himself out of it before Shari and Lola came in, and by the time they did, he was sitting down, the book called *A Friend for Fluffers* open on his lap.

Lola slid into bed, turning on her side to face

him, Page trying to claw her way up. Shari laughed
and put the kitten on the bed and she curled up on
the covers beside Lola and closed her eyes.

Nothing's ever easy, he thought. *Even the easiest thing in the world.*

He only got two pages in when he looked over
at Lola and realized she was sleeping.

"Am I a bad bedtime storyteller or was she
zonked?" he whispered to Shari.

"Definitely zonked. Evy mentioned she'd had
an active day in the park."

Shari turned off the lamp and they quietly left,
leaving the door ajar.

"You're so good with kids," she said. "I spend
all day with children and parents and caregivers,
and trust me, you have a special touch."

"Once I thought I'd be a really great dad," he
said. "But that's done with." He felt his face burn
as he realized he'd said that aloud. What the hell
was wrong with him?

Then again, maybe it was a good thing he had
said it. Even when Felix wasn't sure how he felt,
if he blurted it out, there it was.

He should get going. The pizza was gone, the
little charge was asleep. And this had gotten awkward as hell because of him.

Shari was looking anywhere but at him. What

he'd said was too charged—for him to elaborate, for her to ask any questions. To respond at all.

Luckily, her phone pinged and took her attention off him. She went into the living room and picked it up off the coffee table. "Oh," she said, her voice a bit squeaky. "Your great-uncle just invited me to Sunday dinner with the Sanchezes. He says it's family tradition and that he'd love for me to join tomorrow night."

Oh, man.

He glanced at her, then down at his feet. What was Stanley doing? Without asking him first? "That sounds like Uncle Stanley. He's an inviter. He said he loved talking to you at the quinceañera and was excited that you're going to order more Spanish language books for the library."

She tilted her head. "So you're okay with me going?"

I don't know, he thought. *No, maybe I'm not. Maybe it's just too much. Too, too much.*

"Let me ask you this, Felix. Would *you* have asked me to go?"

Honesty, he remembered. Best policy.

"Probably not," he said. "Because that implies something I'm not ready to imply."

That was honest. Maybe too much.

"That we're a couple," she said.

"Right."

"I know we're not, Felix. And even if we were, you just said you're done with the idea of having children when it's something I want more than anything."

He stared at her—hard. She was handing him his out right there. Both their outs. But...

But what? Why was everything in his head, in his heart a damned *but*?

"So I guess we're back to being friends," she said—stiffly.

But that's not what I want, either.

"Look," he said. "Whatever we are, I would like you to join us for dinner. You *are* my friend, no matter what. And now the entire Sanchez clan adores you." Trying to uninvite her would get even more awkward than the last ten minutes had gotten.

"Who knew pizza and bedtime stories could get so fraught?" she asked, her voice heavy, her expression sad.

Dammit. This definitely wasn't what he wanted. To hurt her.

"I'll see you tomorrow night," he said. "I'll pick you up. Six okay?"

"Six would be great."

So now they were kind of back to being friends but she was attending his weekly family dinner.

And no matter how causal the Sanchez Sunday

dinners were, that he was bringing someone was a big deal. And everyone would know it.

Including Felix.

Chapter Thirteen

At four o'clock on Sunday, Felix had an appointment with Winona Cobbs at Wisdom by Winona, which operated out of her great-grandson's Bronco Ghost Tours business. Sundays were always popular for tours, and a big group was just leaving as Felix arrived.

Follow the moon and stars, Winona had said.

Felix went down the hall. A purple door stenciled with moon and stars had to be the one.

He knocked. He'd purposely made the meeting time close enough to the family dinner so that he'd be anxious enough to ask real questions. Hard questions. But still give him enough time to decompress before he had to pick up Shari.

The door opened and there was Winona, not smiling or frowning, wearing a purple turban on her head, and a purple velvet dress.

"Right this way," she said, directing him into the room and to a table with two chairs, one purple, one pink. She gestured at the pink one, and he sat down.

He got right to it. "My wife died three years ago. Cancer," he said. "The first year, I was a grieving mess. The second year, just kind of going through the motions. This year, I've felt a little more like myself, but aware of this heaviness inside me. Like a stone right here," he added, tapping his chest.

Winona nodded. She didn't say anything and continued to stare at him with that same completely neutral expression.

"I haven't dated. Haven't been interested. But then I ran into someone I knew back in high school and we got to talking. The night you and my great-uncle—the night you gave Stanley a reading at Doug's."

She nodded again and still said nothing.

"Shari's the first woman I've been interested in. The first woman I've been attracted to. And there's something really there between us. But—"

More staring. The expression didn't budge.

"But…" *I can't go through that again*, he thought. That was really it. That was the *but*.

"I loved Victoria so much. I was so excited for our future—for the baby we were planning on. And then just like that, a diagnosis. And she's gone. Our plans are gone. I'm gone. I guess I don't see the point in letting myself love someone again."

This time, Winona's expression did change, just a bit, but Felix caught it. A flash of fire in her dark eyes. It made him stop to think about what Winona had been through. A teenager in love. Sent away when she got pregnant. Lied to by her parents that the baby was stillborn when actually, she had been adopted out to another family. And left in so much pain that she was institutionalized for a time. Not until a couple years ago had Winona been reunited with her child because of Josiah Abernathy, who'd never given up on finding their baby who he'd known was alive and out there somewhere.

If after all that betrayal, heartache, separation and hope, Winona saw the point in falling for Stanley Sanchez, then why couldn't Felix see it for himself with Shari?

"What if you already love someone?" Winona asked.

He narrowed his eyes. "I didn't say anything about loving Shari. We're just…" Something.

"You know what they say, Felix. You can't stop progress."

He frowned. He'd just poured out his soul to her and that was what she had to say? The oldest cliché in the book?

Winona continued to stare at him. "There will come a point when you'll know which way to go."

"Which way is that?" he asked.

"You'll know."

This was just too frustrating. "Can you at least tell me what the ways are?"

"I'll be honest, Felix. I don't tell people that they're going to meet a tall, dark stranger. Or that their next girlfriend's name will start with *B*. Teen-aged girls like hearing stuff like that. What I know I *feel*. So I'll tell you this. There are two ways for you to go. One way is to Shari. The other is to nothing."

He frowned again. "Nothing? It's either Shari or nothing?"

Winona reached up her thin arms to adjust her turban. "If you let Shari go, you're choosing noth-ing over her. That's what I mean."

No. Winona wasn't right. Psychically gifted or not. "*Or* I'm choosing to wait until I'm ready. Com-pletely ready. I mean, is it fair to hold back in a re-lationship? Is it fair to not give all of myself? Is it fair to take a step forward then two back? That's not how I want to treat Shari. She deserves—" He let out a heavy sigh and clamped his lips shut.

She deserved much better than that.

"You're very conflicted, Felix Sanchez, so I'll add this—as I said, you can't stop progress. Progress is what you feel for Shari. Even if you don't know what that is exactly. Or what you want. The opposite of progress is stagnancy. Nothing."

Felix didn't like this reading. At all.

"Can you give me the teenaged girl's reading?" he asked.

That got a smile from Winona's beautiful, lined face. "I guess your burning question needs to be *why* stagnancy—and I know you've had years and years of education, but I do suggest you look up that word in the dictionary and a thesaurus—is even an option in this particular scenario."

This was *not* the teenaged girl's reading. He frowned and let out a breath. "So my burning question is why I might choose stagnancy over Shari Lormand?"

She nodded and stood. "I'll see you at dinner," she added, leading the way to the door.

Well, if Winona had conspired with her beau to invite Shari to the family dinner and then push him into Shari's arms with this beyond frustrating psychic reading, mission accomplished. Because right now, Felix really needed a damned hug.

You'd think Felix's sister Camilla would want to take a break from the kitchen when she owned a restaurant, but nope, there she was at the stove, insisting their mom and dad, who loved making their big Sunday dinners, relax in the living room with the family while she took care of making the enchiladas. It was just after five o'clock, so only Camilla was here so far. The rest of the group would arrive at six.

"Put me to work," he told his sister. Her long dark hair was in a ponytail, and she wore their mom's apron, which was hot pink with Chez Sanchez imprinted in silver, a stocking stuffer from the five kids years ago.

"Wait, *you* want to help cook?" she asked, turning her big brown eyes on him. She'd already made what looked like fifty enchiladas, the sauce, both red and mole, simmering on the stove. A big pot of fragrant rice was also cooking.

"Sure," he said. "I can pour tortilla chips in a bowl or something."

Camilla laughed. "That you can. And you can tell me what's on your mind. Because I know something is."

He sighed. "Let me ask you a question," he said, reaching into the cabinet for five bags of tortilla chips. His great-uncle had made his incredible salsas this morning so at least Felix didn't have to start chopping green chiles. "How would you define the word *stagnancy*? And what would you say are synonyms?"

Camilla eyed him for a second, then reached for the pan of red sauce and poured it onto the enchiladas in the two baking dishes. "Stagnancy. I guess at its core, it means stuck. Not moving—and certainly not forward.

Felix thought about her definition as he poured the mole sauce over the next two baking dishes of enchiladas as his sister had done with the red sauce. Camilla opened the oven and he slid them in.

"But can't stagnancy be a good thing?" he asked. "Don't people meditate to be still?"

Camilla reached into the high-tiered basket of vegetables and fruits and pulled out several avocados. Even in his jumbled state of mind, he was already anticipating Camilla's homemade guacamole. "Well, meditation is forward-moving. It's not about stagnancy at all. It's about letting your mind clear, to be in touch with yourself and your mind and your emotions and your body."

Oh.

"Felix, if you want to know what I think…"

"I do."

"After you lost Victoria, you weren't stagnant," she said. "Think about it. You were actively grieving. Then you were finding your way back to your life in a world without the woman you thought you'd spend forever with. You moved back home and have been a big help to Mom and Dad, you got back to work, you added volunteer hours at Happy Hearts Animal Sanctuary. But until recently…"

He watched his sister slice the avocados in half and scoop out the pits. "Until recently?"

"For a while there, yeah, I'd say you were stuck, Felix. Not because of inability, but because of unwillingness, and there is a difference. But not lately. I'd call making out with Shari Lormand at the quinceañera moving forward, brother dear. I'd call not coming home that night moving forward."

He narrowed his eyes. "How'd you hear about that?"

She only laughed and began mashing the avocado in a big orange bowl.

"I still don't feel ready, though," he said.

"For?" she asked.

"Giving in to what I'm feeling for her. Yes, I have strong feelings for Shari. But seventy-five percent of me doesn't want to act on them."

"The ole head versus heart."

He nodded. "Winona says I'd be choosing stagnancy over Shari. That I should be asking myself why."

"Do you know why?"

He shook his head. "Do you?"

She gave him a gentle smile. "Maybe because it's really scary to put yourself and your heart out there again. To love someone again. After what you've been through. The three quarters of you that doesn't want to act on your feelings is probably about that."

He knew she was right. He'd always known that.

The front door opened and closed and Felix was pretty sure he heard his soon-to-be brother-in-law Boone Dalton's voice.

"Mmm, something smells amazing!"

Yup, that was Boone.

"Do not eat all the guacamole this time," his sister Sofia said on a laugh as they both came into the kitchen.

Perfect timing, too. Because this conversation was making his head spin.

Shari knew just about everyone at the Sanchez family dinner because she'd met them at the quinceañera, but she'd seen them in town or at the library at some point or another over the past three years. There were Denise and Aaron, Felix's parents, and Stanley and Winona, who once again was decked out in purple, this time a pantsuit. Felix's sister Camilla and her husband, Jordan Taylor, were at the far end of the long rectangular dining table. Shari knew that Jordan's family, one of the wealthiest in Bronco Heights, owned Taylor Beef. In fact, it was the Taylor family who'd donated the beautiful, grand building that housed the town library.

Felix's other sister, Sofia, and her fiancé, Boone Dalton, were across from the Taylors. Boone was also from a wealthy ranching family, but the Daltons were relatively new to town. Next to Sofia and Boone were Felix's two younger brothers, Dante and Dylan, and at this moment, Denise was telling both that she had a double date in mind for them, the twin daughters of her newest client. These two Sanchez brothers were as good-looking as their older brother. Both hadn't hit it off with any of the women Denise had had in mind for them at the quinceañera, much to their mother's dismay. Still, she'd never give up.

"We can find our own dates," Dylan said, heaping yellow rice onto his plate next to four enchiladas. "But thanks."

"I saw a photo," Denise singsonged. "Both lovely."

"Fix-ups rarely work out," Dante said. "And what if the date is a disaster? Then your client is pissed and never comes back to the salon."

"I'd rather you and Dylan were happily settled down than I keep a client, even if she does spent a fortune on lowlighting and extensions."

"All in good time," Winona said suddenly, and all eyes swung to her.

"Yeah, all in good time," Dylan said, giving his mother a pointed look.

Shari took a bite of the enchilada with mole sauce and almost sighed with how delicious it was. "Wow, this is beyond delicious, Camilla."

"Thank you. Your date helped me cook."

Shari smiled at Felix. "Scrumptious. I've never had rice this soft or flavorful."

"That's Camilla," Felix said. "All I did was put the pans in the oven. She wouldn't even let me slice an avocado."

As the family laughed and talked and ate and told stories, Shari so aware of her gorgeous date beside her, an unexpected wistfulness to be part of this family came over her. She'd love to attend the mandatory dinner every Sunday. She imagined herself pregnant, Felix rushing her to the hospital at the tail end of a Sunday dinner, the entire family crowding in the waiting room to find out if it's a boy or a girl.

The feeling that she was being watched shook her out of her little fantasy, and when she glanced up, Winona was staring at her.

That sharp dark-eyed gaze, all the life and experience in that lovely ninety-five-year-old face, made Shari face facts.

Once I thought I'd be a really great dad. But that's done with.

Just the thought of what Felix had said triggered the same sharp ache in her chest now as when he'd said it. And how he'd said he wouldn't have asked her to go with him to this very dinner because of what it implied.

That we're a couple, Shari had said.

Right.

I know we're not. And even if we were, you just said you're done with the idea of having children when it's something I want more than anything.

So I guess we're back to being friends.

And because they'd slept together and he was a good guy, he'd wanted to come over with pizza the next night and clear the air, which they had.

They were friends.

There wasn't going to be a serious relationship with Felix Sanchez. She wasn't going to be rushed to the hospital with her extended family of in-laws awaiting the birth of their child. She was once again waiting for something that wasn't going to happen. Putting someone else's needs and wants before her own.

Shari was here not because Felix had invited her, but because his great-uncle had.

Oh, Shari, wake up, girl. Face facts. Don't be stupid.

When she got home tonight, she'd take a long, hot soak in a bubble bath, focus her mind on what she wanted that she *could* have, and go from there.

And she couldn't have Felix Sanchez so it was time to let this dream go.

As Winona had said: *just do.*

By the time the last enchilada was gone and the five different desserts gobbled up, Shari's heart couldn't take much more of this. Stanley and Winona had left to attend one of Evan Cruise's ghost tours. Sofia and Boone were on their way out, and Denise and Aaron resisted all Shari's offers to help clean up.

"You two go enjoy a walk around the neighborhood or have a drink at Doug's," Aaron said.

"Actually," she whispered as they headed out after goodbyes and hugs with the Sanchezes, "I'm ready to get home."

He tilted his head. "Oh. Okay. Are you feeling all right?"

"Not really," she said. "Here," she added, tapping her heart.

His face fell. "Ah. My fault."

"Not your fault. You were always honest. I've been hoping for a different outcome, but I need to accept that you can't make promises."

"Shari, I—" He turned away for a moment, then looked back at her.

"Well, you can't. And I have big dreams, Felix. I want a family. I want a child. I started looking into my options and then we… And I thought *maybe*. But you can't even commit to dating me, Felix."

He was quiet for a long moment. "I wish I could give you everything you want. But I'm not…"

"Ready."

He just wasn't there. He might like her a lot. He might be very attracted. But he wasn't available. And she had to let herself go.

"Can we be friends?" he asked. "And I mean that. Real friends."

Because it's that easy to spend time with someone you're in love with when they just want to be buddies. She'd thought she could handle it because she cared about him and they were already friends. But this back-and-forth, trying to be okay with "going with the flow" when they were kissing on dance floors or having sex in her bed and then trying to be okay with just being friends… Well, she couldn't really be okay with either. The former would lead her only to the broken heart of all broken hearts. And the latter would be painful even when they were at their most playful and happiest, naming a new litter of stray puppies or something.

Either way, she was doomed.

And now she kind of understood how he was feeling. Unsure and unsettled.

"Of course," she said. Because she did care about Felix.

"Good."

And then he drove her home and instead of wondering if he might kiss her as she would have before their awful conversation, she smiled, thanked him for the nice evening, which killed her to say, and then got out of his truck and ran inside.

To a waiting Page. Thank God for cats.

As she stripped off her clothes and drew a bath, she sat on the edge of the tub with her iPad and searched for "foster parent" and "Montana" and "Bronco County." She hadn't explored that route to motherhood yet. Tonight, she would.

By the time she got out of the tub, she'd put the idea of becoming a foster mother and adopting through that channel at the top of the list. There were so many children who needed loving homes.

She couldn't have what she wanted most of all, she thought—the man she loved. But she could have a family. She could create what she wanted.

As she slid on her terry robe, Page sniffing her lavender-scented ankles, Shari was well aware that when she pictured a little boy or girl in the living room, building a block tower or doing a little dance, Felix was there, too.

Now it was Winona's words that came back to her. *You know what to do. Do that.*

She didn't anymore. Because she didn't want a family without Felix Sanchez beside her. And he didn't want a family at all. Or a relationship.

No, Shari didn't know what to do at all.

Chapter Fourteen

Monday: Felix texted a comment about the weather and a rain cloud emoji. And that was it.

Tuesday: Felix texted that he was at the diner, trying to decide between a meatball parm sub or the Thanksgiving club—including stuffing and cranberry sauce—and had she ever tried the club? She reported back that she had, twice, actually, and it was pure comfort, leaving out that it reminded of her last Thanksgiving, a real bust. She hadn't flown to Denver to spend the holiday with her parents because her father had had the flu. So she'd been alone but embarrassed to say anything. Evy and Lola had spent the day with Doug's family, Jemma had gone to Las Vegas to meet her three sisters for their annual family tradition, and so Shari had had cereal for dinner and gone to bed early. Sometimes, being single was great. And sometimes it was the worst. P.S. He didn't ask if he could pick her up lunch and drop it by the library.

Wednesday: Felix texted that a calf, Snowball, he'd been worried about pulled through and would be fine. Champagne emoji. For a minute she'd thought he was inviting her to celebrate with him and stared at her phone like an idiot for the next hour, awaiting the ping. But that had been the only text from him.

Thursday: Felix texted that one of his furry patients from the shelter had a litter of kittens and maybe once Page was medically cleared and the kittens weaned and ready for adoption, they could pair Page up with a buddy. Shari sent back a Definitely! Everyone can use a buddy!

Because she was who she was, she'd fretted about that last part for the next few hours. Would he think she was being sarcastic? Was she? But because Felix was who he was, and she was getting to know him pretty well, she doubted he'd read anything at all into the text.

Friday: Felix texted to ask how that night's grand opening of Evy's new boutique, Cimarron

Rose, was. He hadn't been able to go due to an emergency at a local ranch. Shari reported back the night had been a smash success and that the Hawkins Sisters, the four rodeo competitors, were there with their mother, Josie, and practically bought out the place. Shari added that she'd spent a lot of money herself for a good cause—her good friend's cash register—and absolutely loved everything she got, including a multi-chain-link belt with dangling little green cactuses, a scented candle called Cowgirl Grit, which she hoped would fill the air of her apartment with determination, and some very interesting bracelets. She didn't add that she'd gotten him the matching candle to hers: Cowboy Grit, which smelled like sandalwood and a little vanilla. She'd give it to him the next time he did her a favor, like when he'd come over to help find Page.

This was good. He was respecting what she'd said about not being able to deal with the one-step-forward two-steps-back approach to their relationship and was keeping his distance, yet still checking in. Every day. Because dammit, she was special to him and she knew it.

She missed him. Everything about him. Two days ago when she hadn't been able to find Page after two hours of searching, she'd almost texted him for help, but having him in her apartment, especially when she was anxious about her beloved little pet, would have made her even more aware of how much she wanted him in her life. Needed him in her life. She'd learned last time Page had gone missing that the kitten was very likely fast asleep somewhere Shari would never have expected. Fifteen minutes later, when Shari had pulled out a book on the bottom shelf of the bookcase, there she was, her tail curled around a mystery novel.

Felix had basically taught her the same principles during their time together. She'd been able to predict some things, such as his kindness, that he'd be there for her. But otherwise, she'd had no idea what to expect.

So it was better this way. Really, it was, she told herself for the hundredth time that week as she now reshelved books on Saturday afternoon in the Children's Room.

"Ooh, your super hot rebound sex guy is here," Haley Butterman whispered, jerking her thumb toward the doorway.

Haley was leaving the library in a week to attend pastry school and Shari couldn't wait until her last day.

"I'll put the rest of these away," Haley added. "Remember to channel Beyoncé," she added on a whisper. "If he likes it he should put a ring on it. Even metaphorically speaking."

Maybe the library could give Haley an early send-off. Or at least stick her in the archives on the third floor for her final week. She'd conspire with Jemma about that.

Shari turned and walked over to meet Felix. He looked so good. It was slightly chilly today, and he wore a black leather jacket and jeans and work boots.

"I have a favor to ask," he said. His expression gave nothing away about seeing her again. He simply seemed…pleasant. As if she were Jemma or any other librarian and not the woman whose heart he broke. Which meant he was working hard for that pleasant expression. She sighed inwardly. "My uncle Stanley says that Winona's feeling under the weather and he'd like to bring her a couple of books. He says she likes to read everything."

"That's thoughtful of him. Hmm, maybe a biography and a mystery."

He nodded. "Sounds good. Could you help me choose?"

She should direct him to Jemma. Before she burst into tears, which she might do at any moment. This was just too much, too hard. But she lifted her chin and composed herself from the inside out. "Well, let's see. There's a recent biography of Amelia Earhart that's gotten great reviews.

And a new cozy mystery series has a female detective named Winona."

"How'd you do that in two seconds?" he asked.

"Trick of the trade. I'll lead the way." The sooner he checked out his books, the sooner she could hurry into the women's restroom to cry in private. But of course she didn't want him to leave at all.

Because she was deeply in love with the guy.

Five minutes later, as they headed to the checkout desk with both books, where Jemma was sitting on her stool, his phone pinged.

"Animal control officer is asking for my help," he said, reading the text. "Hikers spotted a stray skinny white dog up near the base of the mountain but the dog was too skittish to go to them, and he can't search for him now. He's on another call."

"I'm off in five minutes," Shari said without thinking. As if thinking would have elicited a different answer. "I'll help."

"Yeah? That would be great."

She felt like he was saying, *Look at us, starting our friendship again after all that...awkwardness, isn't this nice?* Or maybe Felix Sanchez was as hurt and confused and sad inside about where they were as she was. *You know that's the case, Shari*, she told herself.

Jemma checked them out and then said, "I'll run

these books to Winona's house on my way home. I live close by. You two go find that poor pup."

Felix smiled. "I appreciate that. I'll let my uncle know."

Jemma took the books, Felix texted his uncle and then they were off. They stopped at the clinic to pick up some treats to lure the dog with, a light blanket just in case he needed to wrap up the dog to carry him, a leash with built-in collar, and a kennel for the cargo area.

Of course, she was too aware of Felix beside her in his SUV. As they drove the fifteen minutes to the mountain and the woods, she veered between being happy to be with him, near him, helping him on this mission, and heart-wrecked about their status as just friends. She had no idea why she'd thought she could be friends with Felix. Was she supposed to yearn and wish and hope every time they were together that he'd feel more for her? Enough to break through the barriers he'd erected?

He parked at the base of the mountain where a well-marked trail led through the woods and to the famed cavern that had served as a hook-up spot for Bronco's teens for generations. The dog might have gone to seek shelter in one of the many nooks and crannies. The farther you went in, the easier it was to hide from anyone.

Shari walked alongside Felix on the two-person

trail, breathing in the beautiful scent of pine and fresh air off the September breeze. She heard a twig snap and turned her head.

"There! I saw a swish of a white tail!" she said.

Felix turned and pointed. "I see it. Let's follow him laterally and when he realizes that we're not chasing him, he may rest. And then hopefully we'll get close enough to lure him with the treats and I can get the leash over his head."

"Got it," she said.

They walked slowly, once or twice brushing against each other.

Shari saw a flash of white again, but it seemed to be heading away from them, not parallel. A wet drop pinged off Shari's forehead. "Uh-oh. Was rain forecasted? I thought it was just supposed to be overcast."

The sky opened up in one of those downpours with very little warning.

"Cavern opening right there," he said. "Let's run for it. I think the dog took off in the opposite direction, but he'll find shelter in these caves, I'm sure. I'll come back in the morning and look for him."

They dashed into the cavern on the side of the mountain. Decades of canoodling in these caves had left thousands of initials carved into the rock walls. Shari could smell the remnants of a fire, but she didn't hear anything or see anyone.

"Could we actually have this place to ourselves?" Felix asked, shaking the rain from his hair. He draped the blanket around her shoulders. "Warm enough?"

"It's a gorgeous evening even with the rain," she said. This couldn't be a more romantic setting, she thought with another inward sigh.

As they walked a bit farther in, searching for the recently stamped-out fire, they found it down a winding path with a nook that hid it from the walkway. Maybe the dog would find it a good place to feel safe and they could get him to the clinic tonight.

Felix grabbed a book of matches from his backpack and relit the pile of partially burnt wood, and in moments, their nook was warm and cozy.

"We'll wait out the rain here," he said. "We might even get lucky and the dog will come right to us because of the warmth."

Shari took off the blanket and laid it down on the ground at a reasonable distance from the fire. "Just what I was thinking," she said.

"Liver snap?" he asked, holding out the baggie with the treats.

She laughed. "Uh, no."

"Kidding. But I do have granola bars and water. And a box of raisins. I actually love raisins."

"Me, too."

They munched the raisins and drank the water, the fire casting the most beautiful glow on Felix's face. Here they were, chatting like…friends.

This might be the last time you see Felix, she thought suddenly. Because this hurt too much. *So just get through it. The bittersweet pain. Be his friend. Let him be yours. For tonight. Then you're going to have to let go.*

"That was so sweet of your uncle to want to bring Winona books when she's not feeling well," she said. "Warms my heart."

"Mine, too."

"Do they see each other often?" she asked.

"Every day. I heard my mother ask him if he thought he was rushing into this new *amor*, but Stanley said at their ages they don't have all the time in the world left. So taking it slow doesn't make a lot of sense to them."

"Aww, I'm so glad they found each other. Every time I catch them around town, they look so happy. You can see the sparkle in their eyes from across the street."

He nodded. "I love seeing my *tio* like this again."

He must want that for you, she wanted to scream, but held back. Felix was who he was, wanted what he wanted, and that was it. The only one who could change his mindset was the man himself. And he wasn't budging.

What maybe hurt most of all was that he'd tried. With her. And had gone back to friends. Yes, she'd told him she couldn't handle the back-and-forth, but he'd chosen friendship over exploring what was between them, taking it slow.

"Ever been to these caves?" he asked.

"Nope. I always wanted to have my first kiss here," she said. "Most of my high school friends did." She looked at him. "Was yours here?"

"My first kiss?" He shook his head. "Stairwell between the first and second floor at Bronco High. On the landing by the window."

She gasped. "Mine, too. With Eric Fieldwalker."

"I remember his bright red hair, but that's about it."

She chuckled. "He constantly chewed peppermint gum. He almost burned my lips once."

Now he was staring at her lips.

And she was staring at his.

Her own thoughts just a few moments ago came rushing back to her.

"I have a proposition for you," she said before she could change her mind.

He waited, looking at her with a mixture of wariness and tenderness.

"I know that being friends with you is just too much for me. I want more and I can't have it, and it's impossible to hang out with you as if there's nothing wrong. Here," she added, patting her chest.

"Shari, I—"

She held up her hand. "Look, we're here, in a cave with a fire burning, no one around, rain pouring outside, and neither of us has ever kissed in the famed kissing cavern of Bronco, Montana. I think we should. As a final goodbye to all that stuff that had been brewing between us. We'll kiss, walk out into the washed air and forest, and we'll go our separate ways."

"Separate ways," he said. "I don't like the sound of that. But I understand."

She nodded.

They were both sitting with their legs crossed. Criss-cross applesauce, as they called it at story time at the library. And they both leaned forward. Maybe they should have discussed the details of the kiss. The last kiss they would have. Because when their lips touched, she felt the singe of his mouth, soft and warm and hungry. They both got up on their knees, one of his hands in her hair, hers around his neck.

"Mmm," she whispered. "Now we're part of Bronco tradition."

"I think a lot more goes on in these caves than

just kissing," he said, staring at her with smoldering hazel eyes.

She put a hand on his chest and just that touch sent chills all over her body. "Maybe we should extend our final hurrah to include more than just kissing, then."

"A final hurrah," he repeated, very slowly nodding. "I think I would like that, Shari."

"Me, too. Even if it feels sad."

He reached out a hand to the side of her face.

I love you so damned much, she thought.

They would make love again. For the last time. And then, as they'd said, they would go their separate ways.

The fire crackled then, which she took as a sign that she could absolutely do this. She was wearing a sweater dress, easy to smush up around her hips, easy to pull down just in case a bunch of teens came wandering through. Felix came closer on his knees, then gently laid her down on the blanket and kissed her, one hand in her hair again, the other pulling up her dress—and pulling down her underwear. She unsnapped and unzipped his pants and pulled them down. There was something *un*romantic enough about this that made it easier to bear.

"Luckily I still have the condom that Stanley put in my wallet," he said, producing it in his hand.

She took it and rolled it on, loving his groan. A groan that helped her focus on what they were doing, not what she was feeling in her chest. *Let yourself go, Shari*, she told herself. *Just give yourself this. One night. One last night with the man you'll always love.*

"A last hurrah," he whispered, his eyes serious on hers.

"A last hurrah," she whispered back and kept her eyes open, wanting to remember everything.

Because they *were* in a cave in late summer on a warm mid-September evening, the rain could still send people inside seeking shelter. She wished she could be naked. She wished they could stay for hours. Take their time. But that wasn't what this was about anyway.

This couldn't be slow and tender. It had to be fast and hot. And that was exactly what it was. He was on top of her, the glow of the fire casting shadows on his gorgeous face, and the moment he thrust inside her, she closed her eyes despite wanting to see everything, to remember the look on his face. But the sensations were just too much, too great, too explosive. They rocked together, both trying to keep their moans to a minimum, Shari biting her fist at one point so she wouldn't scream in ecstasy and bring other cave-lovers running to her aid.

She'd need aid later. Not right now.

She opened her eyes to find Felix's beautiful hazel eyes looking at her. And then it was over all too soon, both of them spent and sated, breathing hard. He held her hand for a moment, then let go.

Just like she'd let him go.

Shari would never forget tonight. It was a good send-off. Painful, but good.

As she wiggled her dress down and he wiggled his pants up, he glanced at the rock walls full of initials.

"I have a pocketknife," he said, reaching into his backpack.

What would he carve into the wall? she wondered, watching as he scooted over on his knees and put the knife into the rock. When he was done and moved to the side so she could see, she grinned.

FS & SL were here.

"I love it," she said. "Old school."

He nodded, his eyes focused on her. She could tell he was searching for the right thing to say.

"You don't have to say anything, Felix. This was perfect. Not perfect in the big-picture sense, but for right now, for us."

"You're an amazing person, Shari Lormand."

"You mean SL," she said, trying so hard not to cry. She stood up, and Felix put everything in the backpack and then tamped out the fire with sand and his boots.

The downpour let up and they waited by the cavern entrance for the drizzle to stop completely. There was no sign of the stray dog. But like Felix said, he'd come back tomorrow morning.

"This was magical," she said. "I'll always remember it and you."

"I wish we could be friends, Shari. But I understand—clearly."

Yes, she knew he understood. "Look, if you need me, I mean *really* need me, I'm there. I'll always be your friend, just from afar. But if you need me, call me."

"Same," he whispered.

How she held in the flood of tears she had no idea. But when he dropped her off at her building, refusing his three offers to walk her up, she ran inside and upstairs into her apartment, then slid down the back of the door and sobbed.

There was another of hour of sunlight, even if overcast, and Felix couldn't bear the thought of going home with his heavy heart or leaving that stray dog out there, probably soaked from the downpour, for a chilly night, so he went back to the woods.

As he walked along the path, keeping watch on

both sides for any flashes of white fur, he couldn't stop picturing Shari's face. And how she'd looked at him just an hour ago when they'd been in the cave. With *everything* in her eyes. Feeling, yearning, desire, lust…maybe even love. It was that last one that had kept him from saying or doing anything beyond what he had, which hadn't been much. Just saying yes to her proposition for their final hurrah.

That look—the love, if that's what it was—had locked him up and all he'd been able to think was that her idea was a good one. One more time and then goodbye. Go their separate ways. It had to be for the best right now.

It just hurt like hell. Finding the dog would help. It'd give him an immediate purpose and soothe his aching chest.

"Hey, pooch," he called softly into the low brush on both sides of the trail. "I have liver snaps. No dog can resist, not even one who's scared and alone."

He stopped and listened. Was that a whisper of rustling to his right? He reached into his pocket for the baggie of treats and took one out so the dog could smell it.

He heard the rustling sound again.

"It's me, actually," a familiar voice called.

He whirled around, shocked to see Shari, in

jeans and a black wool sweater and hiking boots, holding a bag of treats in one hand and a leash with a collar in the other.

"I couldn't bear the thought of him being out here alone and hungry and scared and soaked," she said.

Oh, Shari. He was speechless for a moment. Of course she was here.

"Same," he said. "You're a very good person, Shari Lormand."

"Just an animal devotee," she said. "Like you."

Another rustling sound could be heard to the left. He turned that way. And saw the flash of white. Yes!

"We're friendly," he called out in a singsong voice. "And have treats. And a warm clinic to take to you so we can get you checked out and then into a foster home and registered with the shelter. Doesn't a soft cozy memory foam bed sound good to you? Regular meals? Belly rubs?"

"Lots of belly rubs," Shari added.

He strained his neck to peer into the brush and around trees and there was the face. Long snout, tall ears. Between small and medium, not more than twenty pounds. And dirty. But a beauty.

"I see him," she whispered. "Aww, what a pretty dog."

"Here, good boy," Felix said, tossing the treat.

He turned to Shari. "Let's sit down to appear less of a potential threat."

They sat. The dog sniffed and tentatively came forward. Then a bit more.

He stopped about ten feet away.

Felix threw another treat so that it would land closer to the dog. The pooch walked to it and sniffed it and then gobbled it up. Then went for the first one Felix had thrown.

"There's more where those two came from," Shari said, tossing another treat at the halfway mark between them.

As the dog took a couple more steps, Felix assessed his demeanor and body posture best he could. Tail was half up, half down, which meant he was wary. His eyes weren't showing slivers of white, which often indicated fear, but neither did he see aggression in the face or stance.

"I have a good feeling about his demeanor," Felix said to Shari. "One more?" he called out and threw another a foot away from himself.

The dog came over and ate it, then just stayed there.

"One more treat," Felix said, "and then we'll see if we can get the leash on you, okay?" He took it from the backpack and set it down beside him so the dog could see it. He threw one more treat just a couple feet from the leash, and the pooch ran to get it.

"Well, hello," Felix said, holding out his hand palm down for the dog to sniff. Again, he didn't see aggression or fear. This dog had likely been someone's pet who'd gotten lost.

Shari held out her hand just as Felix had. The dog sniffed hers too, his tail slightly wagging.

Felix let him sniff him some more and then gave him a scratch-rub under his chin. The dog instantly relaxed. "Yup, just as I thought. A good boy. Let's get the leash on you and we'll go to the clinic and get you checked out and see if you're chipped. And we'll get you a better meal. Sound good?" Still seated, he slipped the rope part of the leash around the dog's neck, which the sweet guy accepted, and he tightened it just the right amount. Relief washed over him.

"Well, this wasn't my favorite day, but it sure has a nice ending," Shari said.

He looked at her and nodded. "Agreed." He wanted to say more. He wanted to do more. Like take her in his arms and just hold her. But he'd just apologize again and that wasn't what she wanted from him.

Felix and Shari gave the pup one more pat each and then they both stood. He slung on his backpack and held firmly to the leash, but as he started walking, the dog walked easily beside him, Shari on the other side.

At the parking area, Shari got down on one knee and petted the dog. "I know you're gonna find a really great home," she said. "You were a trouper up there. You were scared and alone and now look at you. About to get a full belly and a fun toy, too."

With that she gave Felix something of a lopsided, sad smile and ran to her car.

"That woman is something special," he told the dog. "But you already know that. Dogs just know."

The dog looked up at him, head tilted as if to say, *And what are you going to do about it?*

Nothing. Just like Winona said. Nothing, nothing, nothing. The word echoed in his head, and he frowned, trying to shake it off. Not that he could.

But I'm not going to think of it as stagnancy. It's just calm. Easy. No risk.

Nothing was just the absence of something, he told himself. That didn't sound dire.

His head and heart a bit more settled, Felix got the dog in the back of his SUV and into the kennel.

A half hour later, because sometimes things *did* work out like in the movies, a family, including eight-year-old sobbing twin boys, came rushing into the clinic to pick up their beloved Scampy, who'd been missing for a week and a half. Felix had found the microchip and had looked up the information in the registry and called the owners. Scampy was in good condition, no injuries, and once back on a good diet, would bounce back very quickly.

Felix headed home feeling a lot better than he had when he'd started up that path to find the stray. He texted Shari that the dog was microchipped and his family had already picked him up, and she sent back a smiley face. There. That was it. The end of their friendship.

As he parked in the driveway, the Sanchez house was dark, which was strange, since Stanley was usually home at this hour, making his prized salsa that he'd put into individual little containers for Denise and Aaron and Felix to take with their lunches, along with a side of tortilla chips that he always special ordered from Mexico.

Felix turned on the light, but then realized one lamp was on in the living room. And Stanley was again sitting on the sofa, a stack of old photo albums on the coffee table. He didn't look happy. Felix walked into the living room and sat next to his uncle. "Tio, are you feeling heavyhearted again?"

Stanley wiped under his eyes and nodded. "I ran into Shari in the supermarket about an hour ago."

"Oh?" Felix said, tilting his head. Must have

been right before she'd decided to head back to the woods.

"She was buying a lot of cat food. I was right behind her in line with my basket of green chiles and tomatoes and that coffee I like."

Somewhere between that and home, Stanley had gotten very upset. What could have happened?

"I invited Shari over for dinner tomorrow night. Told her I was making my award-winning salsa and that I'd also make black bean and cheese quesadillas with whatever her favorite filling was. And, Felix, her eyes filled with tears and she said she appreciated the invitation, but that you two had gone your separate ways."

He glanced away, trying not to think of Shari in line at the grocery store with tears in her eyes.

"I told her I was very sorry to hear that. And on the drive home, all I could think about was Celia and how wrong it is that I'm seeing someone else now. It's just wrong. If it's wrong for you after three years, it's wrong for me after just one. So I pulled over on the side of the road and I called up Winona and I told her I was very sorry, but I just couldn't do this."

Oh, Tio. No.

"Stanley," Felix said, "just because I'm not ready for a relationship doesn't mean you're not. I mean, clearly you are."

Stanley shook his head. "It's not right. Winona is so wonderful. So funny and smart and full of sass. So many stories. I could listen to her talk all day and night. And when we kiss, it's like fireworks are going off over our heads. But I had my great love and that was enough for one lifetime."

"But you have such strong feelings for Winona and you enjoy her company," Felix said. "There's no reason to stop dating her."

Stanley shook his head. "After Shari left the grocery store, I realized why you're choosing to be alone over a relationship with that lovely woman who you clearly have deep feelings for. And all of a sudden, I started to shake. I realized you're absolutely right."

Felix swallowed. "I'm right? What do you mean?"

"I can't go through another loss. I just can't. Winona means too much to me. I need to just be on my own. I have my family and my salsa and my mariachi music and Doug's once a week—that's enough for me. I'll be on my own, just like you."

With that, his uncle stood up, his eyes redrimmed and teary. He straightened his leather vest and practically ran into his room down the hall.

Oh, no, Felix thought, his head dropping down. Wasn't he just thinking earlier when he was looking for the stray dog that some things worked out like in the movies?

How the hell am I going to fix this?

Chapter Fifteen

Monday morning, Shari was at the library, giving a young patron his very first library card, which always called for celebration. The boy not only got his card but two stickers. Little moments like this at work helped her forget her personal life, which had her so heavyhearted she was surprised she wasn't tipping over constantly. Ten times last night she'd picked up her phone to text Felix to ask more about the dog's owners, what his name was, if there were kids in the family. But she'd put the phone down. His text about finding the owners was short and sweet, just to let her know the dog's story had a happy ending. Unlike theirs. She had to let it go at that.

She looked at the proud little boy holding his library card and smiling up at his dad, and that warmed her heart to the point that even she could smile as the pair left.

Then the smile faded.

Sadie Chamberlin, the woman who'd been in a couple of weeks ago to look up information about her late brother-in-law, Bobby Stone, came in, looking pale and nervous. She was carrying two books, which she set on the counter. "Hi, Shari. Just returning these."

"You okay, Sadie? Honestly, you look like you've seen a ghost."

"That's a perfect description," Sadie said, tossing her long blond ponytail behind her shoulder. "But it wasn't me who saw a ghost—it was one of my neighbors. She said she could swear she saw Bobby carrying a bunch of papers in the park while she was walking her dog last night. Then this morning, when she took her dog to the park again, she told me she found a couple of flyers about Bobby Stone blowing around." She frowned. "Could Bobby still be alive?"

Shari didn't know every detail about what happened to Bobby Stone, but it seemed clear to everyone that he'd died. He'd sat on the haunted barstool at Doug's and then had fallen to his death off that mountain ledge three years ago. It was a tragic accident. A man in good health in his thirties. But rumor said he'd been drinking and lost his footing. Shari felt terrible for him, especially anytime she was in Doug's and saw that awful cordoned-off Death Seat.

"Wouldn't he just let people know?"

Sadie bit her lip. "I don't know. I don't know what to think anymore."

"Your neighbor must have been mistaken, that's all. It was dark, right? Maybe it was just someone who reminded her of Bobby."

"Maybe," Sadie said. She sighed and glanced up at the clock on the wall. "I'd better get going. Thanks for listening, again."

As Sadie left, Shari checked in the books she was returning. *Are Ghosts Real?* And *True Tales of Haunted Places*. In a town that had a booming ghost tours business, the idea of ghosts and haunted places being real wasn't all that far-fetched.

Shari recalled the stone being thrown through the window at Doug's back in July with the note on it: *A Stone You Won't Forget*. And the flyers saying *Remember Bobby Stone* going up all over the rodeo last month. Now, someone thought they actually saw the man in the park.

Shari didn't know what was going on but she hoped Sadie would find some peace.

She set the books on the return cart and was very glad Haley Butterman wasn't around to take the cart up to the adult floor because Felix Sanchez had just walked in the library—and Haley would definitely have something to say.

Shari's heart fluttered at the sight of him. He wore a light gray button-down shirt and charcoal pants and his black leather jacket. What was he doing here, though?

"Remember you said that if I really needed you, I could call you?" he asked, his expression grim.

"You must *really* need me if you're here in person, then," she said. What could be going on?

"Can we talk?" he asked.

"Of course." She led him over to the wing chairs in a recessed area by the stairs. They sat down and Felix dropped his head in his hands.

"Oh, boy. What happened?" she asked.

"It's my uncle. He broke up with Winona. And it's my fault. He's following my lead."

She felt her eyes widen. "Oh, no. Did I have something to do with that?" She frowned, a pang hitting her hard in the chest. "I ran into him in the grocery store before I headed out to the woods to look for the stray. Stanley so kindly invited me to dinner and I was in a…mood, so I guess I blurted out that we're not in each other's lives anymore. Ugh, I'm so sorry, Felix."

"No, no, Shari. It's not your fault. He told me last night that he realized I'm right—that he's too afraid of ever going through the hell he went through when he lost my great-aunt Celia. That he understands why I'm on my own and that he should be, too."

"But he shouldn't be." *And neither should you.*

He leaned his head back. "I know. What can I do to fix this? Stanley wouldn't talk to me anymore last night. He just stayed in his room. I knocked, but he wouldn't answer. And this morning, he didn't come down to breakfast and then when I came knocking on his door again, he told me he would be okay eventually and to please give him some space. Stanley never wants space."

Shari wracked her brain for an idea, but kept coming up empty. "I'm trying to think, but beyond flat-out lying and pretending we're a couple, I don't know how to get them back together."

Felix leaned back against the chair. "But maybe the four of us can get together? Have dinner at your place?"

"For what purpose, though?" she asked.

He let out a breath. "I don't know. Just to talk it out?"

"I'm not sure there's anything to talk out, Felix. You said Stanley was following your lead. You're afraid to put your heart on the line again. So why shouldn't Stanley be?"

"But he can't give up the woman he loves because he's afraid of losing her."

She was about to say *You are.* But Felix had never said anything about loving her.

"All that matters is how he feels about Winona, not what I'm doing or not doing!" he said, exasperation in his voice and expression.

"Hmm," she said, sliding her glasses up on her nose. "Okay. I'll invite them. I'll tell them both that we'd like to apologize for our relationship getting in the way of their relationship. Which is true." Maybe it would help somehow. It was worth a try. "We'd be getting them together in the same room, talking openly and honestly. Maybe it'll make a difference in Stanley's mindset."

He looked so relieved. "Thank you, Shari."

She pulled her phone from her pocket. She pressed in Winona's number.

"Hello, dear," came Winona's voice.

"Winona, I'd like to invite you over to dinner at my apartment tomorrow night to talk things over. Felix is calling Stanley to invite him right now."

"What time, dear?"

Shari's shoulders slumped with relief. No questions, no nothing. Perfect. "Six o'clock?"

"I'll be there," Winona said. "But only because

I know exactly what's going to happen. So nothing will be too big a surprise."

Shari swallowed.

What was going to happen?

"Winona, could you give me an idea of what to expect?" Shari asked.

"See you tomorrow at six, dear," Winona said and then disconnected the call.

Shari bit her lip and told Felix what Winona had said.

His hazel eyes widened. "What's going to happen?"

"I don't know. And now I'm kind of nervous."

"Me, too," he said. He took out his phone, called his uncle and invited him to Shari's place. "She's invited Winona and it's a yes from her." He stared at Shari and crossed his fingers. Shari could just faintly hear Stanley's reply, peppered with Spanish, coming from the phone. Felix was listening and listening. "I know…Yes…No…Yes, I know. But will you come?" More Spanish. More listening. "Yes, but will you come, Tio? Tomorrow at six?" More listening, then Felix flashed her a thumbs-up and something of a smile. "Oh, good. No, you don't need to bring anything." He rattled off Shari's address. "See you at six."

"Phew," he said. "At least we've got them in the

same place at the same time. I feel sort of good about this."

She gave him a commiserating smile. "Me, too. Hopeful."

She wished she could say as much about them.

"What should I make for dinner?" she asked.

"I don't want to put you to any trouble. I'll bring takeout from the Italian restaurant Pastabilities. I know they love that place."

A night when Shari wouldn't have to make herself dinner for one along with Page's little bowl of Fancy Feast? Oh, yeah—she was in.

"Shall I order you your favorite entrée? Linguini carbonara with a side of garlic bread, right?"

She inwardly sighed that he remembered from the one conversation they'd had about favorites— and at the thought of once again being able to eat all the garlic bread she wanted without worry about kissing afterward. There would be no more kisses with Felix Sanchez. "Exactly that."

"Done," he said. "I already know Winona's favorites because Stanley has talked nonstop about her the past couple of weeks. I know her favorite kind of soda, cocktail, color, songs—you name it."

"Aww, we definitely have to get those two back together. We *have* to, Felix."

He nodded. "We do. But no matter what, thank

you, Shari. I don't know what I would do without you."

You're going to find out, though, aren't you? And you're okay with that.

She turned away before her eyes could get as misty as they felt. And when he left, she watched him go and really did think the heaviness of her heart would tip her over any second.

At 5:30 p.m. the next night, Shari set the table in her dining nook, opting for pretty candlesticks that wouldn't obstruct anyone's view of the other guests. Felix was bringing the food, Uncle Stanley insisted on bringing his favorite dessert, tres leches cake, and Winona was bringing a bottle of both red and white wines. That left Shari to be a very free hostess who could concentrate on the room— the emotions, the expressions, the conversation.

At five forty-five, she went into the bedroom to check herself out in the full-length mirror in the corner. She wore one of her favorite dresses—the one with the circles and squares that had accompanied her to Felix's house that night she'd spent in his bedroom. That seemed very long ago. This time she didn't pair it with the book necklace that Felix had liked so much. Instead, she went with her horseshoe pendant since horseshoes were all about good luck. She pushed her glasses up on her nose, smoothed back an errant curl, and sent up a silent prayer for the best for tonight.

For the happiness of a very dear elderly couple.

The buzzer rang. It was Felix. She opened the door and almost gasped at how good he looked. He always did, but something about him tonight, in a dark green sweater and dark pants, black leather shoes, and the black leather jacket she found so sexy, had her absolutely rapt for a moment. In one hand he held a bouquet of roses, white, pink and red, and in the other a huge bag containing their meal. Page came over to rub against his pants leg and he reached down to pet her.

Unless she was imagining it, his gaze lingered on her dress. "You wore that the night we sat next to each other at Doug's," he said.

She nodded, but didn't respond. She'd rooted around in her closet for what to wear tonight, this important occasion, and the moment her eyes hit the dress, she knew it was the one. That night had been magical in its own way. The dress would always be special to her, always remind her of Felix. To the point that she probably wouldn't wear it again after tonight.

"The flowers are so beautiful, thank you," she said, taking the bouquet into the kitchen to put them in a vase. She knew they weren't for her, but for the dinner itself.

He followed her inside and put the bag from the Italian restaurant on the counter, then started removing containers. "They're for you," he said as if he could read her mind. "The flowers. Just my way to say an extra thank-you for doing this. Helping me out. Helping out Stanley. And Winona."

"Of course," she said. "Love is everything."

Did he wince? Or had she imagined that?

"How did Stanley seem today?" she hurried to ask as she took out plates and bowls and a basket for the Italian bread.

"Down in the dumps." Felix's shoulders slumped. "I called him a couple times to check in, but he didn't say more than two words."

"Poor Stanley. I can't bear to even imagine that sweet, vibrant man sad for one second. We've got to get him and Winona back together."

He nodded. "I'm just not sure how."

By taking a risk yourself, Felix Sanchez. That's how. By showing Stanley that the great-nephew he loves so much is willing to give someone his heart. "Let's see where the conversation goes."

When the buzzer rang again, Felix went to the door while Shari ladled out the food onto plates and bowls and brought out the dishes to the table. The redolent food was still steaming.

"Stairs can't best me," Winona said, stepping onto the landing. She wore a purple coat with silver trim and silver Mary Janes, her white shoulder-length hair gleaming. Stanley was behind her, looking dapper in his leather vest and Western shirt, black pants and cowboy boots, a black Stetson on his head.

Shari grinned. "They get me when I have to run back up when I forget something I need, which is always when I'm already blocks away." She held open the door for the two to come in, then took Winona's coat and Stanley's hat, hanging both in the closet. "Welcome. Please have a seat. You and Winona are here and here," she added, pointing to the two chairs on one side of the table.

Felix sat across from his uncle and Shari took the seat across from Winona.

Winona glanced down at her plate. "Oh, goodie. I just love spaghetti Bolognese." She twirled a forkful. "Mmm, just delicious. Did you know that Stanley took me to the Italian restaurant for our first date?" She put her fork down and looked at Stanley. "I sure do miss you, Stanley."

Stanley pushed his chicken piccata around on his plate and sheepishly glanced up at Winona, his expression so sad.

Shari glanced at Felix. He seemed to be searching for just the right thing to say.

"I know that my uncle misses you too, Winona," Felix said. "This whole thing is my fault."

Stanley sat like a rock, eyes downcast, his expression glum.

"What do you mean, dear?" Winona asked.

"I tried to explain to Stanley that just because I'm not ready for a relationship doesn't mean *he's* not ready," Felix said. "Clearly, he is ready." He tried for a smile, looking between Winona and Felix.

Stanley shook his head. "Oh, it's not about being ready."

"Isn't it?" Felix asked.

"It's about being unwilling to go through the heartache again," Stanley said. "Who can handle that more than once? Not me. Not you, Felix—and now I understand. I'm sorry I tried to fix you up with all those women I ran into in the supermarket. What a fool I was. No one needs to go through what we both went through twice."

"Are you saying I should never date again?" Felix asked, staring intensely at his uncle. "That doesn't sound like you."

"It doesn't sound like the old me," Stanley explained. "The new me knows better now. Better to be like you. You always say you have your work and your family. I have my family and my salsa. And my mariachi and the weekly true crime podcast I like." He looked up at Winona. "I'm so sorry. You're such an amazing woman. But this is what

I need to do. I admire my grand-nephew and how he lives his life. I'm going to follow his lead. And be alone."

"But, Tio," Felix said.

All eyes swung to him.

"But what?" Stanley asked.

Felix sat up straighter and looked pointedly at Stanley. "You don't want me to ever have another relationship? Ever? Because that's what you're saying."

Stanley shrugged. "Well, maybe just with women you're not really interested in. No one you'd fall for. Like Shari. I mean, that's why you're not a couple, right? You like her too much."

Felix glanced at Shari. "I do like her. Very much."

"I know," Stanley said, cutting a piece of his chicken piccata. "That's why you decided you can't have a romantic relationship with her. It's too much. The potential heartache."

Felix tilted his head. "*Potential* is the key word there, though. Potential means maybe, not definitely."

"But then why aren't you and Shari a serious couple?" Stanley asked.

Now it was Felix who was staring at his plate. "Because... I'm not ready."

"For?" Winona asked, her dark gaze on his.

"A relationship," Felix finally said.

Winona took a piece of Italian bread from the basket. "May I ask why?"

"Because..." Felix stammered a bit, clamped his lips shut, then responded. "Because of what Stanley just said. Who needs to go through that heartache again?"

"So you *are* ready for a relationship," Winona said. "You just don't ever want to feel the way you did when you lost your wife. Is that right?"

Felix looked at Winona, then at Stanley, then back to Winona. "I don't want to feel that way. No. And to avoid feeling that way ever again, I don't date."

"Except you kind of dated Shari," Winona said.

"Kind of," Shari added—unnecessarily.

Felix gave something of a nod. "But we realized a romantic relationship wasn't right for either of us. I'm not...in the market. And Shari has hopes for her future that I can't give her."

She felt the weight of sadness in his words and wanted to cover his hand with hers, show him some support, but she took a sip of wine instead.

"Ah, but you just told Stanley he shouldn't hang his hat on the word *potential*," Winona put in. "You don't know you'd feel that same heartache. Nothing is guaranteed—we all know that. I mean, I suppose Stanley knows that I won't be around forever. I plan to live until I'm one hundred and twelve, by the way."

Stanley brightened.

"At Doug's," Winona said, staring at Felix, "when you and Stanley came to my table for a reading, I said your life was an open book, but there was nothing there for me to read. That's not the case anymore."

Now Shari felt herself brighten. Not that she understood what Winona meant exactly. But it sounded like back then, everyone knew Felix Sanchez was a widower who didn't date—*open book, nothing to read here, folks.* But now, he'd opened up his life a bit to include Shari, even if it was just pieces, false starts. They'd made love twice. That was big for Felix. He'd let her inside and then needed to shut her out. Except for the safety of friendship. And Shari had been the one unable to handle that. Felix's life had changed. He was changing. And change did not come easy.

"You can?" Felix asked—warily. "What do you see?"

Winona narrowed her gaze on him. She nodded slowly. Then nodded again. "Oh my."

"Oh my what?" Felix asked.

But Winona returned her attention to her food and didn't look up at Felix even though he kept trying to catch her eye.

"What does she mean?" Felix leaned close to Shari and whispered. "'Oh my'?"

"I'm not sure," Shari whispered back. *Oh my* could mean anything.

Once everyone had pushed their plates up a bit, just crumbs left, Stanley stood up. "This was a mistake. I'm sorry, Winona. But Felix is right. I adore you, but I can't see you anymore. I just can't risk it. I can't lose again. I'm so sorry," he added, tears misting in his dark brown eyes. He turned to Felix and Shari. "Please see Winona home. It's just too painful for me to be around her anymore." Then he rushed out the door, forgetting his hat.

Winona's eyes filled up with tears. She stood. "I'd like to go home."

Shari glanced at Felix, about to burst into tears herself. "We'll take you right now."

Felix stood. "I feel so bad. Just terrible. This isn't what I wanted. This wasn't how it was supposed to go."

"Like I said, nothing comes with a guarantee," Winona said to Felix. "Tonight proved that. But at least you tried. Trying is all we can do."

"Can I wrap up the cake for you?" Shari asked Winona.

"Oh, yes, please," Winona said. "My heart is broken and the cake will make me think of Stanley and tonight, but I like reminders of my deepest feelings. It means I feel. That I care. That I love. And that's everything. Even after all I've been through."

Shari glanced at Felix, hoping Winona's beautiful pronouncement would get through. But he just looked upset, stony, his hazel eyes downcast.

Now what?

Chapter Sixteen

Shari and Felix walked Winona to the home she shared with her daughter and granddaughter and she hurried inside and practically closed the door in their faces. Felix let out a groan. That wasn't a good sign. Not that anything tonight had been, but he'd been hoping she'd have some wisdom to impart. That she knew something they didn't.

Shari sighed as a lock clicked from inside. "She's had enough of us, for sure."

"Yeah," he said. "We didn't exactly fix anything." He leaned his head back and stared up at the dusky sky. "I wish I knew how to get through to Stanley."

"You could always take your own advice," she said as they walked toward his SUV.

"That advice applies to Stanley, not to me."

Shari put her hands on her hips. "So you really think it's better for you and only you to be on your own than with someone you have strong feelings for because you know you could lose that person at any minute?"

"Why risk it, Shari? And it's not like *I'm* deciding this."

She stopped walking. "What? Who is, then?"

"I mean," he said, "that it doesn't feel like a choice I'm making. It's just the way I feel. Here," he said, slamming his palm against his chest.

"Fight for me," she said, lifting her chin, her eyes blazing. "Fight for me and fight for Stanley's happiness."

"What?" he asked.

"That's right. Fight for me, Felix. If you have strong feelings for me, if you want me in your life, if I'm special to you, if for the first time since your loss you feel something big, then fight for me. For us. And in doing so, you'll be giving your uncle a gift. Love. Winona. And the peace that comes from knowing that his beloved grand-nephew is happy."

He turned away, looking out toward the stand of trees across the street. "Maybe a few days away from his love will make Stanley realize he can't bear to be apart from Winona. He has to come to that himself."

"It hasn't worked for you," she said, her voice heavy. "And that's how I know it *is* a choice you're making. You're deliberately shutting me out of your life to protect yourself. And I do understand why, Felix. You went through absolute hell. But we found each other. You might not have been looking for me, but there I was, there *we* were, and what's between us has a life of its own."

The neckline of his sweater felt like it was squeezing him. His ears were clogged. His chest was tight, the muscles of his shoulders bunching. He looked at Shari, this beautiful, wonderful woman who did have him all turned around, but he…couldn't. "I'm sorry, Shari. I know I keep saying that. But I am sorry."

"No, I'm the one who's sorry. And Stanley and Winona. You're just…stuck. And you want to stay stuck."

With that, she turned and walked with slumped shoulders to his SUV, getting in the passenger side.

He got in too and started the engine. "Shari—"

"Unless you're going to tell me that you've had enough of being stuck, of turning away the most fundamental thing in the world, I don't want to hear it. You heard what Winona said. There are no guarantees in life. But can you tell me you would rather not have loved and lost than never have loved at all?"

He didn't say anything. He started the car and pulled away, driving in silence.

He'd hurt Shari. He'd hurt his uncle and Winona.

He'd hurt himself.

And there was nothing he could do about it.

After a terrible night's sleep, Felix threw off the blanket at the crack of dawn, the sky still a hazy pink-yellow, and figured he'd make a cup of coffee, then go ask his uncle the question that had been bothering him all night. When he entered the kitchen, he found Stanley working on his salsa. But there was no pep in his step as there usually was when he made salsa. No mariachi music. His shoulders seemed slumped, his face more lined. Or maybe it was just the unusual sight of his uncle's heavy frown. Stanley Sanchez was a smiler. Except lately.

Thanks to Felix.

Stanley didn't even have the energy to say good morning. He just gave Felix a nod and pointed at the coffeemaker, which was full.

Felix got out a mug and poured a cup, adding cream and sugar. "Uncle Stanley, let me ask you something," he said, leaning against the counter on the other side of the chopping board where Tio was hard at work on tomatoes.

"Okay." Chop, chop, chop.

"Do you believe it's better to have loved and lost than never to have loved at all?" Felix asked.

Stanley turned to him and put down his knife. "What kind of question is that? Of course I do."

Felix slugged down half the mug of coffee. "I'm not sure I can say the same."

Stanley Sanchez let out a string of curses in Spanish, waving his hands in the air. To the point that Felix's parents had come rushing out of the rooms in their bathrobes and were halfway down the stairs, stopping when they saw Felix was with Stanley. They stayed put, clearly wanting to eavesdrop on whatever Felix had said to make his uncle so upset.

He was doing that a lot these days.

"Let me ask *you* something, Felix," his uncle said angrily. "Given what you went through—starting with Victoria's diagnosis. The loss of your dreams to start a family. The knowing that she was going to die. The year of hell while she fought. And then the night you had to say goodbye to the woman you'd spent half your life with. Your wife. Your heart and soul. Given all that, would you rather have never known Victoria? Never loved her?"

"Of course not!" Felix ground out. "What kind of question is that?"

"What do you think you just asked me?" Stanley said. "What do you think we're talking about?"

Felix froze. He stared at his uncle, something inside Felix clicking—as if he suddenly understood.

He wouldn't have given up his life with Victoria to have avoided the pain of losing her. Of course he wouldn't have.

And he shouldn't give up his chance for happiness with Shari out of fear—which had had a death-grip on him—that he could lose her, too.

He would rather *love*.

He *did* love. He loved Shari Lormand. With everything he was. With all his heart.

"Oh, my God, Tio," he said. "I didn't understand. I've always known that phrase. Everyone knows that phrase. But I never really thought about it until just now. I didn't even think about it last night when Shari threw it at me."

"Threw it?" Stanley said, shaking his head. "She asked you the right question, but you didn't have the answer. Now you do."

He remembered going silent right afterward,

turning away. Starting the car and dropping her off. Everything in him stagnant. Nothing.

"I would rather have loved and lost than never have loved at all," Felix said, grabbing his uncle into a fierce hug. *I would*, he thought.

Stanley hugged him back hard. Felix could hear his mother crying—her happy tears—and his father whispering that everything was going to be okay now.

Maybe everything was.

"I get it now, Uncle Stanley. I finally get it."

"I'll believe it when I see you and Shari together. I'll know it by your faces if you said what that woman needs to hear you say."

Felix smiled. "I'm going, I'm going."

He just hoped that Shari would listen. That he wasn't too late.

"Wait," Stanley said with a wistful gleam in his eye. "Come with me first." Stanley turned and headed toward his room. "There's something I want you to have. Just in case it's the right time."

Felix glanced at his parents still on the stairs, and they hurried down, wiping their tears, and following him, their curiosity clear on their faces.

And thirty seconds later, peering into Stanley's room as he handed Felix something very special, they both gasped, their hands over their hearts.

* * *

"What do you think, Page?" Shari asked, holding up her black sweater dress and her tweed pantsuit.

Page walked onto Shari's foot and sat down, half on her toes and half on the rug in front of her closet. How Shari managed to laugh, given how utterly awful she felt, was something. But that was a pet for you. Pure joy. She scooped up the kitten and snuggled her.

"The black sweater dress, it is. I am mourning something, so it's fitting, right? Right." She slid the dress over her head, the medium-weight soft wool instantly comforting. She'd add her book necklace to liven it up. Maybe her black suede knee-length boots since the forecast didn't call for rain and it was getting cool enough for boots finally.

She put on the necklace, which instantly reminded her of Felix. She'd worn it the night she'd sat down beside him in Doug's. The night he'd switched places so he'd be closer to the haunted barstool. The night he'd been ditched by his wily great-uncle who'd left with a date. The night he'd had a little too much to drink and she'd driven him home. The night they'd kissed and fooled around to the point that she'd been down to her bra and underwear—and he'd been in those incredibly sexy boxer briefs. The night she'd been trapped in his room till morning.

The night that had started it all.

He'd told her how much he liked her book necklace.

And now that it was around her neck, the colorful little ceramic books against the black wool, Felix's face flashed into her mind, and she felt a pang in her chest so sharp she staggered backward and had to find the edge of the bed to sit down. And breathe.

She could so vividly picture Winona taking the tres leches cake home with her the night that her own love had turned his back on their love. What had she said? *My heart is broken...but I like reminders of my deepest feelings. It means I feel. That I care. That I love. And that's everything.*

Oh, Winona. You are so right. You've been right all along. I did show Felix who I was and that was all I could do. Same for you.

Today she would call Winona and invite her to lunch. Two gals with heavy hearts. Broken hearts. Getting through.

Her phone pinged.

Shari's eyes widened when she saw it was Winona Cobbs.

The diner has my favorite kind of quiche on special today. Lunch at 1. If you're free.

Shari stared at the text, then looked at Page and held out the phone to the kitten. "Do you see this? I'm not imagining it, right? The woman really is psychic."

She texted back that she loved all quiche and would see her there at one.

Oh, goodie, Winona typed back with a smiley face emoji.

The front door buzzed, and Shari practically jumped. She didn't get many visitors at barely eight in the morning.

"Maybe it's Winona," she told Page. "She definitely is gifted so she knows I'm really sad and she's come to give me a hug. Not that Winona seems the hugging type."

She went to the door and pressed the intercom. "Hello?"

"It's Felix."

Felix. Here. Very early. If he was bringing her coffee and a scone, she'd throw it at him. The scone, not the coffee. If he was going to apologize, she'd... She'd interrupt him and tell him she knew he was sorry, so was she, and they should start going their separate ways immediately because if they didn't, she'd burst into tears and she'd just put on her makeup for work. She'd cry on and off all day, no doubt, but now she didn't want Felix Sanchez's last memory of her to be her looking like a raccoon.

Shari opened the front door and he was right there, as if he'd jogged up. He looked…energized. Not like a man here to apologize. He also didn't have coffee or a bag from Bronco Java and Juice.

"You're the literary one here," he said, "So I did have to look up the quote you asked me last night—about whether I think it's better to have loved and lost than never to have loved at all. Turns out Alfred, Lord Tennyson, nineteenth-century English poet, says it is. And I do, too. My answer is yes, Shari."

She felt her mouth slightly open in surprise.

"I'm not the same guy I was last night. My uncle had to knock some sense into me. You should hear that man curse in Spanish."

She smiled, but it didn't last long because her heart was still hovering between *please be here to say you love me* and *what if he's here to say he gets it now, but he's still not ready*? He'd be ready for the next woman—like her ex had been.

"I knew you were special that first night at Doug's. That there was something so big between us. But I couldn't get out of my head, out of my own way. I got used to my life being one way.

But then how I feel about you blew that out of the water."

"How do you feel?" she asked.

"I love you. I love you so much, Shari."

She couldn't help the gasp that slipped between her lips. Everything she'd longed to hear, to believe, had just come out of his mouth.

"I can't live my life being afraid of risk and loss," he said. "Thank you for showing me that." He took her hand and held it, an electric current zapping up her arm.

This was real. This was happening.

"I want to give you everything you dream of, Shari. I want us to have that dream together. I *am* ready. I was ready the minute we sat down on those stools and shared those chicken wings. I just didn't know it."

"I'm pretty sure Winona did," Shari said with a smile."

Felix laughed. "Yes, both of them. And someone else. My great-uncle Stanley. He knew."

"He definitely knew," Shari agreed with a smile.

"I love you," he said. "And if I'm not too late, if I haven't driven you away, I'd like to show you how much." He got down on one knee, Page instantly jumping on that knee. "Excuse me, Page, if you don't mind, I'm trying to do something here."

Shari was too much in shock to speak or move.

She kept her gaze on Felix's face, which was equally serious and tender.

He reached into the pocket of his black leather jacket and pulled out a small black velvet box. When he opened it, Shari's hand flew to her mouth.

"My uncle gave me this ring. It was the diamond ring he proposed to Celia with sixty years ago."

Shari's eyes filled with tears. "It's so beautiful. And so symbolic of everything love is."

"Will you marry me, Shari?"

"Yes!" she whispered and then dropped to her knees and threw her arms around him, knocking them—and the kitten—over. "I love you too, Felix. So much."

"And it turns out that this is the way to get my uncle and Winona back together. He wants proof that I've seen the light. This ring on your finger and the happiness on our faces will do the job."

She held up her left hand, the exquisite diamond ring twinkling on her finger. This might feel like a dream for days to come. Shari knew she'd be floating around Bronco, floating around the library.

She leaned close and kissed him and he kissed her back with all the pent-up love and passion that had been brewing for weeks.

"Let's go to your house right now," she said. "As another famous saying goes, I want forever to start right away."

"Me, too," he said, pulling her into an embrace. He pulled back to look at her. "Including starting a family. A baby."

Shari gasped. "I love you so much, Felix Sanchez."

"I love you, too," he said and kissed her all the way up to the bedroom.

When Felix and Shari arrived at the Sanchez home, the house was quiet. His parents had both left for work, and Felix didn't see Stanley or hear him humming or singing. His great-uncle had helped change his entire world, and Felix couldn't wait to show him his ring on Shari's finger. The shooting star was in that ring—both of them. Love was in the ring. The future was in the ring.

Felix understood now.

"Maybe he's out back," Felix said as they moved through the living room.

It was a beautiful late September morning. Bright blue skies, seventy degrees and just a hint of humidity to remind them all of summer. He held Shari's hand as they headed toward the sliding glass doors, open to let the warm breezy air flow though the screens. He glanced at the ring again—the ring that symbolized everything he felt for Shari Lormand.

As they were about to turn the corner, Felix

could hear Stanley's voice. He was outside on the deck with Winona. They were seated on chaises, facing toward the yard, a carafe of coffee and a plate of crumb cake between them.

"My sneaky plan worked on that stubborn nephew of mine," Stanley was saying. "If you hadn't been so sure, I wouldn't have been able to go through with it. I didn't want to even pretend that I had said goodbye to you, Winona."

Felix gasped, something he rarely did.

Two lined faced turned toward the sound.

"Busted," Winona said, her expression ever neutral.

Stanley stood up and put out his hand for Winona; she stood up, too. "Okay, you caught us, you two. But Felix, I wasn't pretending when I told you about the shooting star. I was conflicted and worried that day. Talking to you about that, being honest with Winona about it, helped me understand what I was feeling. But if you think I'd follow your lead to be alone when I have this amazing woman in my life, you're *loco*!"

They all burst into laughter, Winona reaching up on tiptoe to kiss Stanley on his cheek.

"I had to help you understand, Felix," Stanley added. "Forgive me?"

Felix pulled his uncle into a hug. "Forgive you?

I *owe* you," he said. "Both of you," he added, smiling at Winona.

"Well, Felix," Shari said with a grin, "we were played, but *well* played."

He laughed and shook his head. "I should have known."

"I did," Winona said, dry as can be. "Oh, and by the way, your ring is beautiful, Shari. Congratulations."

Shari's eyes misted with happy tears. She held up her left hand. Stanley wrapped his arms around her and welcomed her to the family.

"Well, we're finally going apple picking," Winona said. "You two have the house to yourself this morning." Hand in hand, the two left, all smiles at their hard work.

Felix picked up his fiancée and carried her upstairs to his room.

"We never finished what we started here that very first night," he said, laying her down on his bed and touching the little red book on her necklace.

One night that had changed his entire life and given him everything.

* * * * *

*Look for the next book in the new
Harlequin Special Edition continuity
Montana Mavericks: Brothers & Broncos*

The Maverick's Marriage Pact
by USA TODAY *bestselling author
Stella Bagwell
On sale October 2022, wherever Harlequin
books and ebooks are sold.*

*And catch up with the previous books
in the series!*
Summer Nights with the Maverick
by New York Times *bestselling author
Christine Rimmer*

In the Ring with the Maverick
by Kathy Douglass

Available now!

#2935 THE MAVERICK'S MARRIAGE PACT

Montana Mavericks: Brothers & Broncos • by Stella Bagwell

To win an inheritance, Maddox John needs to get married as quickly as possible. But can he find a woman to marry him for all the wrong reasons?

#2936 THE RIVALS OF CASPER ROAD

Garnet Run • by Roan Parrish

When heartbroken Bram Larkspur finds out the street he's just moved onto has a Halloween decorating contest, he thinks it's a great way to meet people. He isn't expecting to meet Zachary Glass, the buttoned-up architect across the street who resents having competition...and whom he's quickly falling for.

#2937 LONDON CALLING

The Friendship Chronicles • by Darby Baham

Robin Johnson has just moved to London after successfully campaigning for a promotion at her job and is in search of a new adventure and love. After several misfires, she finally meets a guy she is attracted to and feels safe with, but can she really give him a chance?

#2938 THE COWGIRL AND THE COUNTRY M.D.

Top Dog Dude Ranch • by Catherine Mann

Dr. Nolan Barnett just gained custody of his two orphaned grandchildren and takes them to the Top Dog Dude Ranch to bond, only to be distracted by the pretty stable manager. Eliza Hubbard just landed her dream job and must focus. However, they soon find the four of them together feels a lot like a family.

#2939 THE MARINE'S CHRISTMAS WISH

The Brands of Montana • by Joanna Sims

Marine captain Noah Brand is temporarily on leave to figure out if his missing ex-girlfriend's daughter is his—and he needs his best friend Shayna Wade's help. Will this Christmas open his eyes to the woman who's been there this whole time?

#2940 HER GOOD-LUCK CHARM

Lucky Stars • by Elizabeth Bevarly

Rory's amnesia makes her reluctant to get close to anyone, including sexy neighbor Felix. But when it becomes clear he's the key to her memory recovery, they have no choice but to stick very close together.

YOU CAN FIND MORE INFORMATION ON UPCOMING HARLEQUIN TITLES, FREE EXCERPTS AND MORE AT HARLEQUIN.COM.

HSECNM0822

He opened the mailbox absently and reached inside.
There should be an issue of *Global Architecture*. But the
moment the mailbox opened, something hit him in the
face. Shocked, he reeled backward. Had a bomb gone
off? Had the world finally ended?

He sputtered and opened his eyes. His mailbox,
the ground around it and presumably he himself were
covered in…glitter?

"What the…?"

"Game on," said a voice over his shoulder, and Zachary
turned to see Bram standing there, grinning.

"You— I— Did you—?"

"You started it," Bram said, nodding toward the
dragon. "But now it's on."

Zachary goggled. Bram had seen him. He'd seen him do something mean-spirited and awful, and had seen it in the context of a prank… He was either very generous or very deluded. And for some reason, Zachary found himself hoping it was the former.

"I'm very, very sorry about the paint. I honestly don't know what possessed me. That is, I wasn't actually possessed. I take responsibility for my actions. Just, I didn't actually think I was going to do it until I did, and then, uh, it was too late. Because I'd done it."

"Yeah, that's usually how that works," Bram agreed. But he still didn't seem angry. He seemed…impish.

"Are you…enjoying this?"

Bram just raised his eyebrows and winked. "Consider us even. For now." Then he took a magazine from his back pocket and handed it to Zachary. *Global Architecture*.

"Thanks."

Bram smiled mysteriously and said, "You never know what I might do next." Then he sauntered back across the street, leaving Zachary a mess of uncertainty and glitter.

Don't miss
The Rivals of Casper Road by Roan Parrish,
available October 2022 wherever
Harlequin Special Edition books and ebooks are sold.

Harlequin.com

HARLEQUIN
PLUS

Announcing a **BRAND-NEW**
multimedia subscription service
for romance fans like you!

Read, Watch and Play.

Experience the easiest way to get
the romance content you crave.

Start your **FREE 7 DAY TRIAL** at
<u>www.harlequinplus.com/freetrial</u>.

HARPLUS0822

HARLEQUIN

Heartfelt or thrilling, passionate or uplifting—Harlequin is more than just happily-ever-after.

With twelve different series to choose from and new books available every month, you are sure to find stories that will move you, uplift you, inspire and delight you.

SIGN UP FOR THE HARLEQUIN NEWSLETTER

Be the first to hear about great new reads and exciting offers!

Harlequin.com/newsletters